# Fireside and Shadow

The Fireside Mysteries: a cozy dragon mystery - book 3

## K.E. O'Connor

K.E. O'Connor Books

FIRESIDE AND SHADOW

ISBN: 978-1-915378-76-7

Written by: K.E. O'Connor

Cover designer: Get Covers

### *The Royal Fallacy: A Dissenter's Perspective*

### *C. Blackthorn*

In the hallowed halls of monarchy, where tradition and pomp reign supreme, dissent is viewed as heresy. Yet, it falls upon voices like mine to shine a light on the dark underbelly of regal authority and the havoc it has wrought upon our realm.

For decades, the Ithric family has wielded power with impunity, cloaking its excesses and injustices beneath a veneer of opulence and tradition. But let us not be deceived by the glittering façade, for behind the gilded walls of the palace lies a legacy of exploitation and oppression.

From conquests to economic manipulation, the royal family has left a trail of devastation, trampling upon the rights and freedoms of those deemed beneath their station. But perhaps the gravest sin of all lies in their role in the death of our dragons.

The sins of the past will not remain buried forever. The dragons have not forgotten the crimes committed against them. And when they rise again, the monarchy will face their fiery wrath.

Don't be beguiled by the glittering spectacles or the false promises. Until we confront the injustices and hold the Ithric family to account for their crimes, we shall forever remain enslaved to their tyranny.

The time has come to rise and reclaim our destiny from the clutches of royal oppression—to forge a new path, guided by the collective will of the people. And when the dragons return to reclaim their rightful place as guardians of our realm, it'll be a reckoning long overdue.

## *A Royal Affair to Remember: Prince Jasper and Camilla's Wedding Set to Dazzle?*

### *From the recently decommissioned Royal Reports*

As the realm anticipates the grandeur of a royal wedding, whispers of trouble within the regal corridors overshadow the excitement. The upcoming nuptials between Prince Jasper and Camilla Oldsbrooke, once heralded as a union of love and a chance for prosperity, face uncertainty as rumors of discord escalate.

Speculation hints at fractures in the unshakeable royal harmony. Prince Jasper, known for his charm, has found his match in Camilla, whose grace and elegance captured his heart. But the romance is under scrutiny as reports suggest tensions brewing behind palace walls.

Sources close to the royal family hint at disagreements and clashes of opinion, fueling fears the couple may be contemplating calling off the ceremony. While palace officials maintain a stoic silence, the rumor mill churns with royal drama.

Adding to the intrigue are whispers of familial rifts and power struggles, with some suggesting longstanding tensions within the royal household are coming to a head. The timing of these rumors couldn't be more precarious, as they grapple with the aftermath of the theft of the dragon statues from inside the castle.

The impending wedding, once heralded as a beacon of hope for the monarchy, has been overshadowed by uncertainty. As we wait with bated breath for answers, one thing remains clear: the allure of royal intrigue shows no signs of waning. Whether the rumors turn out to be gossip or indicators of deeper unrest, the realm's eyes are focused on the royal family, eagerly awaiting the next chapter in this unfolding saga.

**Do you think the wedding will go ahead?**

Send comments to our office in Market Square. And, just for fun, we're having a ball bet! Head to the square and place a red ball in the bucket if you think the wedding will go ahead or a blue ball if you think it will be canceled!

Balls will be provided. And remember, it's just for fun.

# Chapter 1

"Calm yourself! Finn's not to be hurt." I inserted myself between a furious, stamping Stormwing and my new angel friend, Finn.

Stormwing's dragon scales glistened in the dappled moonlight filtering through the treetops in the enchanted glade that currently concealed them. "He should be hurt. This quivering mass of feathers stole a dragon egg. He deserves to be ground to worm food. Although I doubt they'd touch him, given how rotten his insides must be."

"Finn's behavior has us questioning his character." Emberthorn stood close to his furious brother, although he wasn't stamping, more curious.

"Enough with trying to blame Finn for what happened to the dragon's egg! We've already said we'll help Juniper get her baby back." My focus was on the smoking, stamping dragon who wanted to destroy Finn, although I risked a glance at Juniper. She was a new addition to our dragon family after we'd rescued her from Prince Godric's deranged clutches. He'd polluted her with dangerous magic and bent her to his will.

She was a stunning yellow dragon, a healing dragon. But she was also a broken dragon, having lost her precious egg. An egg Finn had accidentally acquired and cared for, rather than doing the responsible thing and returning it to the dragons.

Despite Stormwing's fury filling the glade with tremors and acrid smoke, Juniper barely responded to his tirade. Her heart was shattered, and she wouldn't survive much longer if she wasn't reunited with her infant.

"Juniper is too distressed to even talk to you." Stormwing lifted his foot again, preparing to make the ground shudder. "I'll deal with this spiteful angel creature and make him sorry he ever looked at her egg."

"This wee bamstopper needs a lesson in manners." My ever-loyal wyvern companion, Hodgepodge, leapt off my shoulder, transforming mid-air to become a giant, scaled beauty. Although he professed to despising being large, now he had the ability to change, he used it more frequently.

I tugged Finn out of the way as Hodgepodge and Stormwing slammed into each other in a showy display of growls, raised scales, and smoke. They did this at least once a day, and I could only be grateful for the enchantment around the hidden glade that concealed sound, preventing anyone from discovering the secret family of dragons living so close to the realm that was trying to destroy them.

"Hodgepodge enjoys these fights." Finn stood comfortably close to me, his white wing feathers brushing my shoulder and his tousled sandy brown hair drooping into his eyes, not at all unsettled that a dragon wanted to squash him.

"I don't know about that. But Hodgepodge will do anything to keep me safe and is always willing to go up against Stormwing when he blusters into one of his regular fury moods."

"I understand why Stormwing is so angry with me. He's protecting his new lady friend. I'd be the same if someone hurt a person I cared about." Finn glanced at me and smiled.

There'd been an unspoken romantic tension between us ever since Finn had arrived in the village. It was early days, and we were getting to know each other, but there was something special about this angel-demon. He stirred feelings in me I hadn't felt for a long time. If only I didn't have a horde of unpredictable dragons to look after and a cruel royal family to hide from, I might have seen where this tension led us. But for now, my focus was getting the surly dragons back where they belonged and not fighting with each other or Finn.

Stormwing roared an objection as Hodgepodge flipped him onto his back and pinned him by the neck.

"Should we lend a hand?" Finn looped a wing toward the fight.

"It's only bluster. Hodgepodge can do real damage if he wants to, but he hasn't even used his teeth." My perfect-scaled companion was always there for me, defending me, and ensuring when the dragons got feisty, they'd be controlled. Although, as I grew accustomed to being their emissary, my magic had resurfaced, and it was stronger than I'd ever felt it. We were forbidden from using powerful spells in the realm, and if anyone was caught using illegal magic by the Ithric family, they received a swift death sentence.

But with the dragons awake and fighting to get back where they belonged, more and more magic stirred in me. It was unsettling, but just like being around Emberthorn and Stormwing every day, I was getting used to it. And when the final showdown with the Ithric family cumulated, I'd need every spell I could muster to defeat them.

"Brother! Unless you want to stay in the dirt all night, admit your defeat to Hodgepodge, so we can get on with matters of importance." Emberthorn nudged Stormwing on the side with his giant head.

"This squib won't defeat me." A huge plume of smoke billowed out of Stormwing's nostrils. "If I were at full strength—"

"If you were at full strength, we'd both have our royal seats back. This bickering gets us nowhere closer to our goal," Emberthorn said. "Hodgepodge, be so kind as to release my fiery-headed brother. If he causes more trouble, I'll deal with him."

"This is worth fighting for." Stormwing struggled ineffectively as Hodgepodge snarled at him. "We're talking about a dragon's egg!"

"And we have every right to be aggrieved, Juniper more so than anyone, but you don't see her snapping and snarling at Finn," Emberthorn said.

"She's got me to do that for her," Stormwing said. "Let me up!"

"It's okay, Hodgie," I said. "Stormwing will behave. He knows we're helping."

Juniper limped over and gently snuffled Stormwing's head, instantly calming him. She was the smallest of the three dragons and still had much healing to do. A lesser dragon would have curled up and died, but Juniper's desire to get her egg back kept her going.

"If I let you up, no more attacking Finn or going anywhere near Bell with those enormous claws and sharp-scaled tail," Hodgepodge said.

"He would never hurt our emissary," Emberthorn said. "Bell is too precious to us."

"She's more precious to me," Hodgepodge said. "And I found her first."

I walked over and leaned against Hodgepodge's large back leg. "We're all family. One way or another, we found each other. It doesn't matter where or when that happened. And family look out for each other."

"This doesn't feel like being looked after," Stormwing grumbled.

I arched an eyebrow. "Being a part of a family also means you're put in your place when you overstep. Stormwing, we understand your anger, but we have a solution to reunite Juniper with her precious baby. You just need to listen to Finn, so you know what's happening."

"Can you really get my baby back?" Juniper's voice was slightly lyrical, with a faint undertone of gravel.

"I'm certain of it." Finn inched closer, keeping a watchful eye on Stormwing, who often lashed out with his tail when feeling spiteful. "It'll take some negotiating, but I promise you, she's safe. And I'm sure she'll be thrilled to be back with you."

"We wouldn't need to do any reuniting if you hadn't stolen Juniper's egg and made yourself a fake family with a creature you had no hope of controlling," Stormwing said.

I resisted the urge to eye roll. "As Finn has explained several times, the egg was abandoned at his sanctuary. He didn't steal it."

"He should have reported it as soon as it was discovered."

"My baby's song must be powerful," Juniper said. "Enthralling an angel is no easy task."

"Finn is a good protector," I said. "Why wouldn't a homeless infant pick him as their caregiver?"

"That's pushing things. We don't know him," Hodgepodge grumbled.

"We know him well enough. Finn loves animals. And he healed you when you wandered off on an adventure without me and got yourself in trouble."

"I'll be the first to admit, I got in over my head with the dragon egg," Finn said. "I was convinced I could look after her on my own, but she grew so quickly and became stronger than me."

"It's fortunate she didn't bite your head off," Emberthorn said. "Infant dragons are more dangerous than my grumpy brother when he's rolled off the wrong side of the hay pile and discovered there's no breakfast ready for him to guzzle down."

"Hodgepodge, get off me, unless you want to be chargrilled, you irritating pile of lizard dung." Stormwing bucked several times, Hodgepodge clinging on for the ride, with no intention of letting him win.

I nodded at Hodgepodge, and he reluctantly released Stormwing, who rolled to his feet, shaking out his enormous tail and wings. He bared his teeth at Hodgepodge and then Finn but settled beside Juniper, his flare of anger gone as quickly as it arrived. Stormwing's moods blew in and out like a tempest wind, while Emberthorn was more relaxed, even occasionally lazy. The dragon brothers were a perfect combination, which was why they'd been so successful when they'd ruled the realm.

"Let's hear your clever plan, then," Stormwing snapped at Finn. "How are you getting Juniper's baby back?"

"I've already put out feelers," Finn said. "And I'm firming a few things up."

Stormwing growled. "Not good enough. Those words mean nothing."

"This task will take time," I said. "We all understand dragon protocol is tricky to step through, and Juniper's baby has settled nicely in her new home. Finn knows what he's doing. And while he's working on that, we'll focus on your return to power and stopping the royal family from doing any more harm."

"Both quests are of equal importance," Emberthorn said. "We must have patience."

"I have no patience left." Stormwing flopped a wing over Juniper, almost covering her in his protective, leathery shield. "I vote we charge the castle now, destroy the toxic Ithric family, and then fly out to collect Juniper's baby. We could be back by tomorrow night and have everything settled."

Juniper ducked out from under his wing, her panicked gaze meeting mine as she shook her head.

"Juniper is still healing," I said soothingly. "And although you're much stronger, you still have a week of potions to get through before Seraphina gives you the all-clear to enter battle."

"I refuse to listen to that monster. Seraphina is poisoning us!" Stormwing said. "I feel worse every time she visits."

"But you look so much better than when I first met you," I said. "When you escaped the castle, you could barely walk or fly, and your scales were dull."

"And let's not talk about the revolting gas problem we all had to live through," Hodgepodge said. "You stunk up the whole forest one day."

Stormwing's scales flushed yellow. "That wasn't me. It must've been a family of skunks who'd taken up residence nearby."

I hid a smile. "You're all stronger now. You gleam and smoke and stamp around like true alpha dragons. We're almost ready to move. And now is a good time to set a plan into motion. The castle is consumed with the royal wedding. It's only ten days away, and the place is in chaos."

"We should do a flyby and incinerate the bride and groom as they say their vows." Stormwing chuckled darkly to himself. "I would be highly amused by that."

"As entertaining as that would be, when we reappear, we must enter calmly," Emberthorn said.

I nodded, giving Stormwing a stern look. "We want the Ithric family to have no option but to accept you back.

When residents of the realm realize you've returned, they'll welcome you with open arms."

"And if the royal family doesn't do the same, their true colors will be revealed," Finn said. "If they refuse to let you rule, everyone will turn against them."

"They're already turning," I said. "Every day, I hear rumors about border unrest. People have had enough. They don't want to be ignored and their problems unheard. The Ithric family's days are numbered."

"Can't come a moment too soon," Emberthorn said. "Balance must be restored, or the realm will crumble, and the people will wither and die."

"So, we're all in agreement?" I asked. "No more fighting, and we focus on the mission, while giving Finn time to make arrangements to get back Juniper's baby."

The dragons grumbled their agreement, and Finn nodded.

"Even if the royal family pretends to accept us back," Stormwing said, "they'll betray us the second they have an opportunity."

"And we'll be ready when they do," I said. "On my emissary's honor, they're never trapping you again."

Stormwing growled. "Just what I need to ruin my already dreadful day. A traitor."

I glanced over my shoulder. Seraphina Poldark trudged toward us, a heavy-looking satchel slung over her shoulder. She'd shown up twice a day for two weeks, giving the dragons healing potions to ensure they were recovered from their many years of confinement. Her magic was extraordinary and melded perfectly with Emberthorn and Stormwing, but its constant use took a withering toll on her health. She looked haggard, wasn't sleeping, and had lost weight, but she refused to give up on the dragons.

"We'll leave you to it," I said to her. "Just be warned, Stormwing is grumpier than usual."

"I heard that." Stormwing's tail swished violently through the air, and he knocked Finn off his feet. "I'm watching you, angel-demon. One wrong move against the infant or any of us, and you're toast."

"I thought I was worm food." Finn ducked as Stormwing's tail lashed out again.

"Hmmm. I should have added a strong sedative to this batch of healing potions," Seraphina murmured as she passed me, giving me a weary smile.

We left her to the dragons, headed to the edge of the enchantment surrounding the forest glade, and stepped through the magic. Woodland sounds hit my ears. The chirping birds and scurrying animal noises sounded alien after being in the bubble of magic that kept the dragons hidden and everything else out. That bubble was necessary to protect them until they were ready to reclaim what was theirs.

"I suppose you've got some genius plan to make sure Stormwing doesn't eat you." Hodgepodge was now perched on my shoulder, back to his usual size.

Finn grinned. "I do. I know the perfect powerful duo to act as a liaison. We're going into the dragons' den with a side order of magical cat and powerful witch as backup."

# Chapter 2

"I'd recognize that straw nest of hair anywhere. Bell Blackthorn, where have you been hiding?" Camilla Oldsbrook yanked on my dark ponytail, almost causing me to choke on my mutton and mustard sandwich.

Hodgepodge vanished under the table and hid under my full skirt, so Camilla wouldn't notice him, but she was too busy tutting over my hair as she styled it with her fingers.

I coughed and swallowed my bite of food. "I've not been hiding anywhere. I have a different routine now the stone chamber is closed to the public."

Camilla swiped at the wooden bench with my napkin to avoid getting dirt on her pristine cream silk gown and then joined me. "I still can't understand why Lady Isolda doesn't put the dragons back. With them gone, there are hardly any visitors coming to the castle."

I focused on my food. "She must have a plan for them."

"I doubt that. But if there is a plan, it's a terrible one. And I heard Lady Isolda crying over her lack of funds. It was such a joyful sound. It made me smile all night, knowing how miserable she was because the money has vanished and she's a public joke." Camilla's pretty elven face crinkled as she snitched her nose.

I glanced around to ensure nobody could overhear us, but everyone seemed focused on their food or engaged in conversations with friends. "Things are changing at the castle."

"Not for the better. I've barely seen you these last two weeks." She pinched the skin on the back of my hand. "I've knocked at your hovel several times, but you're never in. What schemes are you plotting? And why don't they involve me?"

"No schemes! And I've started a new job at the castle, so you'll see more of me." I wasn't sure how I felt about my new position. I'd been content cleaning the chamber and looking after the dragons when they'd been trapped in stone, but this role came with a dangerous edge. I was working in the family's private collection room. A collection room full of illicitly gathered powerful magical items.

"Have you been given a promotion?" Camilla asked.

I shrugged. "Still cleaning."

"How dreary. I should have asked you to be my personal maid. None of the staff I requested from my family's estate have yet to arrive." Camilla took half of my sandwich, looked at the contents, then put it back. "I've sent several messages to see what's causing the delay, but I've yet to receive a reply. I expect my letters are being read and destroyed. It would be just the spiteful sort of thing Lady Isolda Yuck Face would do. Mean old hag."

I didn't disagree. Even though Camilla was supposed to marry Prince Jasper Ithric soon and provide royal heirs, Lady Isolda watched Camilla like a vicious bird of prey waiting to pounce on a playful mouse and tear it apart.

Camilla sighed and primped her blonde curls. "I have to make do with one of Lady Isolda's maids, and I don't trust her. I caught her snooping through my closet the other day. When I confronted her, she said she was picking my outfit for that evening's dinner. That was a lie. We'd done that together in the morning, so I knew she was prying into my private affairs."

I was glad Camilla didn't trust the household staff. They were employed because they never questioned orders, no matter how far those orders bent the rules, and I was certain Lady Isolda had Camilla under constant scrutiny. The longer she stayed at the castle, the more erratic her behavior became, and anyone not sticking to the rules got into trouble or vanished, never to be seen again.

"I've been working on something important." Camilla glanced around and giggled. "It's a secret, but I'll share it with you, if you promise not to tell a soul."

"Who would I tell?"

"Friends. Family. Your boyfriend."

"I don't have many friends. No family. And you know I'm not dating."

Camilla jutted out her bottom lip. "If only you made an effort with your looks, someone would have you. For your age, you're not dreadful to look at. And you're always polite."

I kept my tone neutral, even though Hodgepodge dug his claws into my leg. He hated when someone insulted me. "It's something I think about every day. What's your secret?"

Camilla drew in a deep breath, her blue eyes sparkling. "A list of the ways I can kill Jasper."

The bite of sandwich I'd just swallowed stuck in my throat, and I drank water to get it to move. "Are you giving that list to him as a wedding gift?"

Camilla burst into laughter. "Wouldn't that be a treat? Can you imagine the look on his pompous face? Maybe it would give him a heart attack and save me the job of finishing him off. Take a look. I've written them down and scored them from one to ten. Ten being the most likely to succeed." She slid a large piece of paper in front of me, full of scribblings.

I concealed it with a hand. "I know you're only doing this as a joke, but it could be taken the wrong way, and if word of this got back to Lady Isolda, you'd get in serious trouble."

Camilla snorted a delicate note of derision. "I'm untouchable. My last physical showed I was perfect. They wouldn't dare do anything to me. Not when everyone is so desperate for a royal baby."

I nodded slowly as my gaze failed to pick out a single infant in the crowded market. It wasn't just a royal baby we needed. Any baby. We hadn't had a birth in the realm since the royal family trapped the dragons.

My attention returned to Camilla. "Even so, Lady Isolda doesn't have a sense of humor. She may not see the funny side of this list."

"Then she's missing out. Did you see the option for poison? I've been wandering around the castle, and it's easy to get. There are even products in the kitchen that could be used. And I was looking around the stables and found a storage shed full of potions. Some of those should do the job."

Camilla was talking too loudly and waving her arms around as she discussed poisoning Prince Jasper. I'd noticed two royal guards following her and was certain they were listening.

"You must be my flower girl," Camilla said.

The abrupt topic shift caught my attention. "Flower girl?"

"Yes! At my dreadful wedding. I have it worked out. We'll disguise you again, and you'll become the beautiful Bellatrix rather than the downtrodden Bell Blackthorn, who always smells of polish and sweat. No one will know who you are. It would be such fun to have you there."

It would be like signing my own death warrant. "Lady Isolda won't accept a last-minute addition to your wedding party, surely. She's controlling everything."

"It's my wedding, so it's my rules," Camilla said with a sniff. "I've had to accept some of her dreary relatives as bridesmaids, so she must compromise if I want a new friend added. And you must meet my sister. Valerie is my bridesmaid. You can stand together. She's plainer than you, so you'll look quite pretty next to her."

"I'm sure all eyes will be on you on the big day. Just as I'm sure your sister is charming."

Her cheeks flushed. "Oh! I didn't mean that. I can be thoughtless when my tongue runs away with me. Don't tell Valerie I said that. She's sensitive about her looks. I should warn you, she's not like me. Or you. She's... different."

"What does that mean?" I was still processing the plain comment, but that was Camilla. She didn't have a decorum filter. Whatever was on her mind, it tumbled out, no matter who was within earshot.

"You'll see when you meet her. Valerie is sweet and obliging. My favorite sister. Well, my only sister, but it's the same thing. Let's go."

"Where are we going?" I looked at my food.

"To meet Valerie! Keep up. And leave that sandwich. It looks horrible."

Camilla's cajoling was drawing attention, so I had to abandon my half-eaten meal. As I stood, I was careful to adjust my oversized bag, so it neatly concealed Hodgepodge, who had squeezed into the large pocket of my gathered underskirt so he wouldn't be seen.

Camilla led us through the castle's main doors, waving gaily at the guards, who stared at her with bemusement. We marched along the vast stone corridor with its cold lines and unwelcoming atmosphere and into the stone chamber.

I took a moment to take it all in. The space had become a giant wedding fair. There were tables covered in flowers, fabric, decorations, and piles of booklets.

"Valerie! I want you to meet someone special." Camilla grabbed my elbow and led me to a skinny, hunched woman of around thirty-five. She had the same pretty, elven appearance as Camilla, although her pale hair was shaped into a cute pixie cut, and one shoulder appeared higher than the other, giving her a hunched back.

She inspected me, her twinkling blue eyes alight with interest, and nodded a greeting.

"Valerie is my wedding savior." Camilla kissed her sister's cheek. "And she's been marvelous in deflecting Lady Isolda. Valerie even found us new places to hide when my monster-in-law is on the warpath and wants to cause me trouble. Which seems to be a daily occurrence. I'm convinced that hag wants me dead."

"Don't say that!" Valerie's gaze shifted to concerned. "Lady Isolda is only being protective of her son."

"Wait until you've spent more time with her, and you'll change your tune. She's a horror."

I wasn't surprised to hear Camilla now had the full measure of the family she was about to marry into. Lady Isolda was a monster dressed in fine gowns and jewels. There was a heart of stone beneath her refined exterior. A heart bent on ruining this realm for her own greedy ends.

"It's nice to meet you," I said to Valerie.

"You too. Camilla's been telling me all about you." Valerie's voice was a soft murmur, as if she didn't want to draw attention by speaking. "And she told me about your visit to the tavern and your fun in the dress shop. I'm glad she has a friend here."

I felt a touch guilty. The friendship hadn't been my choice, but given Camilla's powerful position, I couldn't refuse or ignore her attention.

Hodgepodge sneezed, and I awkwardly covered it with a fake sneeze of my own. "Sorry! Flower allergies."

"You can't have an allergy to flowers! Not if you're to be my flower girl," Camilla said. "Although you are a bit old to be a flower girl. Flower matron? No, that sounds dreary. Flower crone? That's even worse."

"How about flower fairy?" Valerie beamed at me. "You look magical with your pale skin and dark hair. Like a character out of a folklore tale."

I returned her sweet smile. "That's kind of you to say."

"Fairy is too twee. I'll think of a suitable title. And my wedding will be a perfect opportunity to find you a suitable husband. All of Jasper's dreary friends are coming, but I'm hopeful there'll be one half-decent man among them," Camilla said. "I'm determined to get you settled. I can't have you living in that cold hovel for the rest of your miserable life."

"My cold hovel is nice, and my life isn't miserable," I said.

"It has no heating. And the entire place is smaller than my bathroom."

"How do you know how big it is? You've never been inside."

"I've stood outside plenty of times, though, waiting for you to come out and try to sneak off." Camilla caught hold of her sister's arm. "Bell keeps secrets. She's never where she's supposed to be. What do you think she gets up to when no one is watching her? Seeing a gentleman friend? Stealing from the family? Dancing with the fae?"

"I promise, I don't hide anything from you." The words tumbled out of me. "I've just been busy."

"Doing what? You're not working." Camilla's eyes narrowed. "Anyone I ask doesn't know where you are, although that shady stable hand with one arm got shifty when I questioned him. It's as if you vanish. I'll send a troop of guards after you if you don't reveal everything right this second."

And Camilla would. She wouldn't do it out of malice, just a deranged sense of curiosity. But her curiosity could ruin the plan to restore Emberthorn and Stormwing to the throne.

"Let's focus on the wedding, shall we?" Valerie discreetly winked at me. "I'm sure Bell isn't deceiving you."

I smiled gratefully at her. My lying skills were dismal, and when Camilla got the bit between her teeth, she was loath to let go until she got answers.

Valerie tensed, and her cheeks drained of color. "I hear Jasper!"

"Quick. We must hide. I've avoided him for days. I'm on a winning streak, and I refuse to break it." Camilla dragged us behind an enormous tower of white balloons, and we crouched together.

A few seconds later, Prince Jasper strode into the chamber, surrounded by nervous looking assistants.

"He's so awful," Camilla whispered. "No one likes him. Everyone can see how fake and creepy he is. And don't get me started on his damp hands and onion breath. How did I end up with such a repugnant husband? Well, I haven't yet, but it's only a matter of time. Revolting."

"Shush," Valerie whispered. "We don't want him to find us."

"You're the older sister. You should be marrying him," Camilla said, a petulant note in her voice.

Valerie shook her head. "I'd take your place if I could, but you were there when Lady Isolda visited. She took one look at me and said I was unsuitable."

Camilla placed a hand on her sister's shoulder. "You're perfect. And lucky not to have to marry into this wretched family. Although not being married means you're stuck at home. I'd find you a position here, but this castle sucks the joy out of everything. You'd hate it."

"It's not the castle that's the problem, but the family living in it," I muttered.

Camilla stared at me in surprise then grinned. "Yes! You're right. Get rid of them, and this place would be charming."

"I don't want to move. I'm happy living with our parents," Valerie said. "I'm content to look after them."

"Even so, you must visit me all the time," Camilla said. "If it weren't for you and Bell, I wouldn't survive this dreary, magicless place."

I wasn't sure Camilla would survive for much longer anyway, given the way she was behaving. Whatever I said, I couldn't silence her obsessive fantasies about annihilating Prince Jasper. Maybe they weren't fantasies. If she planned to go through with it, I wouldn't be able to stop her. Did I even want to? Prince Jasper was as bad as his dead brother and almost as twisted as his unstable, cruel mother. Would one less member of the Ithric family cause anyone grief?

"He's leaving." Camilla blew out a breath as she peeked around the balloons. "He's shown no interest in the wedding. He only wants to marry me so he can get me in his bed."

The sisters made gagging noises and then giggled, making them appear young and far too vulnerable to stay in this castle.

"I should go," I said. "It was good to meet you, Valerie."

"You too. See you at the wedding?"

I nodded as I hurried away. I couldn't get entangled in Camilla's bizarre wedding day. Although I had to pretend everything was normal, my focus was on the dragons' upcoming return. It was an event that would overshadow Prince Jasper and Camilla's special day in ways no one could anticipate.

# Chapter 3

My working days had changed dramatically since the dragons escaped the castle. Once the stone chamber closed, visitor numbers had dwindled, despite the Ithric family opening previously private rooms for public inspection, in the hope it would encourage curious locals to spend a few coins to see inside.

But I still had tasks to complete. Tasks that were deadlier than my previous cleaning role.

"Behave today. You almost broke an enchanted vase yesterday and released the magic." I kept my voice low, since it was a busy afternoon in the castle, and there were more people around to notice Hodgepodge and report him to the family as an oddity.

"I was entertaining myself." Hodgepodge hid in a small backpack I carried, which was open so he could peek out and get plenty of air. "The dragons were much more interesting to be around, and I could eat some of the offerings the visitors left. You can't eat dust and cobwebs."

"You always complained about the visitors," I murmured.

"Now I'm complaining because you're surrounded by hundreds of dangerously magical items that could explode at any second."

"If you stay away from them, you won't activate them," I said. "No lifting lids or sniffing unlabeled dried bags of herbs. Those herbs could turn you into a two-headed beastie."

"So much powerful magic in one place is dangerous," Hodgepodge said. "The family clearly has no interest in using it. Most if it is covered in years of grime."

"If they have it, it means no one can use it against them. Now, you need to be quiet. We're almost there."

We were approaching the collection room. As always, they guarded the door around the clock, and someone observed me while I cleaned. Fortunately, the guard monitoring my every move was Warwick Woodsbane.

I greeted the guard outside the door, and he unlocked it and let me in before shutting it behind me with a firm click of the key and a shimmer of magic.

Warwick was already inside the room, sitting at a desk he'd taken over, cleaning the magic staff he carried everywhere. For those who didn't know him, he looked terrifying in an outfit of leather and steel, his dark eyes missing nothing, but there was more to the tough, weathered exterior than most people realized.

He was halfway through his lunch, and Hodgepodge was quick to sidle out of the bag and scuttle to the small pile of grapes left on the side of Warwick's plate.

"Your creature never asks." Although Warwick scowled at Hodgepodge, now I'd gotten to know him, I realized scowling was his default expression. When he wanted to look mean, his expression turned to downright terrifying.

"Hodgepodge knows you always leave him a treat at lunchtime." I pulled my bucket of supplies out of the closet and set them on the floor.

"And he makes such a mess." Warwick slid the paperwork he'd been looking at away from Hodgepodge, who was on his third grape, his cheeks bulging and juice dripping off his chin.

I pulled out a duster and a bottle of silver polish. "I thought I'd work on the pewter and the silver urns."

"Whatever you think is best. I'm no cleaning expert," Warwick said. "I'm assigned to make sure you steal nothing. I have strict orders to watch every move you make and permission to destroy you if I think you're acting oddly."

"That won't happen, since we're on the same side." I glanced at Warwick. He'd been a loyal Ithric guard for a long time, and I occasionally wondered if he'd change allegiances and return to Lady Isolda's cause. But he remained committed to ensuring the dragons return to power, even if that meant working with a castle cleaner and her greedy, grape stealing wyvern.

He smirked. "The only side I'm on is my own. I want out of this role, but while Lady Isolda remains in charge, I'm going nowhere."

"You don't want to remain a soldier once the dragons are back?"

"I'm undecided. Maybe I'll retire."

"And do what?"

"Sleep? Eat too much and get a beer gut? Who knows?"

I smiled at his careless tone. Warwick never made a move without having a plan in place. "I can't see you enjoying retirement."

"I enjoy peace. I've not had that for a long time."

"Have you been to the forest recently?" Along with Warwick, there were several others helping the dragons. Seraphina administered the magic to restore their power and strength. Astrid Nightshade and Evander Thorne checked in on them, along with Griffin, Warwick, and me. We had a roster, so the dragons were never alone for long.

I imagined they found our presence stifling, but we had to ensure they were protected. And as their emissary, it was my duty to keep them safe until they were back where they belonged.

"I stopped by late last night after Lady Isolda went to bed." Warwick flipped over a page and glared at the words. "I wasn't sure I'd be able to get away. She's being... difficult."

"More so than usual?" Hodgepodge chewed on his final grape.

Warwick nodded.

"What kept her up so late?" I asked.

"Plotting. She knows the dragons are out there, but she has no clue where to look. Our lady hates to lose control of a situation. She's taking her rage out on my soldiers."

Hodgepodge swallowed his mouthful of food and jumped off the table.

I selected a silver pewter and set it on the table in front of Warwick. We held our hands an inch from the object. Cleaning in the collection room wasn't as straightforward as cleaning in the stone chamber. Every item contained magic, and some of that magic was dangerous. We had to check each item before I worked on it to ensure, as Hodgepodge said, nothing exploded.

"Feels safe to me," Warwick said. "Are you getting any unpleasant vibes?"

"Nothing." It was a treat to use my powers daily. The more I used them, the stronger they became. Sometimes, the magic felt like it wanted to burst out of me in a scatter of shimmer and sparkles.

"Then get to cleaning." Warwick sat back in his seat. "Lady Isolda is becoming paranoid, more so than ever before. She trusts no one, and she's questioning everyone's loyalty."

"Even yours?"

"Everyone. She's considering making my guards work in pairs, so none of us are on our own. She wants to turn my soldiers against each other and become spies." He growled out his disapproval.

"That won't be good for you," I said. "If you have a shadow, you won't be able to visit the dragons."

"I'll figure a workaround if it comes to it," Warwick said. "Lady Isolda considers me an asset, but that could change in a heartbeat."

"We won't have to do this for much longer," I said. "Seraphina has almost finished healing the dragons. And now Juniper's here, they grow stronger daily. Her energy is something else."

"It was a stroke of luck Prince Godric captured a healing dragon," Warwick said. "Thanks to his handiwork, we can push forward with the plans faster than anticipated. Who'd have thought that sick individual would actually help us bring down his mother?"

I held up the pewter. "It's about the only good thing he's ever done for us."

"Now, we only need to worry about his deranged mother and his deeply unpleasant brother," Warwick said. "Prince Jasper is still being unkind to Camilla. I passed his chambers last night and heard them arguing."

"I met Camilla earlier today. She showed me a list of ways she wants to kill Prince Jasper. It wouldn't surprise me if she goes through with it."

Warwick hissed out air. "You must keep out of her business."

"I'm trying!" I slid him a glance.

"Bell. What are you hiding?"

"Camilla asked me to be a flower girl at the wedding."

Warwick drew in a sharp breath. "You can't draw attention to yourself. You're too valuable to the dragons."

"I said no, but you know what Camilla is like. She gets an idea into her head, and it's impossible to dislodge."

There was a clatter, and I turned to discover Hodgepodge had knocked over an urn, spilling ash across the floor.

"That wasn't me!" He scuttled away. "I was just sniffing it because it vibrated, and I wanted to make sure nothing would come out and attack you."

I hurried over and inspected the urn. "Hodgepodge! This is a funeral urn. That's someone's remains on the floor."

"Sweep them up and put them back in," Hodgepodge said.

"It's disrespectful to use a broom to clean up someone's ashes." I looked over at Warwick.

He shrugged. "They're dead. They're hardly going to object."

The ashes lifted off the floor and swirled to my eye level. Hodgepodge raced over and jumped on my shoulder. He hissed at the swirling ash and swung his tail through it. Warwick was also by my side, the staff he'd been cleaning now sparking with powerful magic.

The ash solidified, and the face of an elderly man with wisps of grey hair, wearing a long white shroud appeared. I stared at him, and he stared back.

"Lord Frederick?" Warwick asked.

The ghostly figure startled, peered at Warwick, and nodded.

"You're Lord Crosby's father?" I asked.

The ghost nodded again, his gaze shifting around the room, taking in his surroundings.

Hodgepodge hissed at him and flared his neck ruff.

"We're not in danger." I pressed a hand against Hodgepodge to calm him. "Are we?"

Lord Frederick paid me no attention as he continued to view the room, his expression puzzled.

"Sorry for knocking over your urn," I said. "We meant no disrespect. If you'd like to return, we can figure out how to get you back inside. Or you swirl back in?"

The ghost coughed several times, each cough getting louder. "No, no. It's good to be out. I don't know how many years I've been trapped in there."

"Trapped? The urn is your final resting place," I said. "You realize you're dead, right?"

Lord Frederick chuckled. "I do. But I didn't die of natural causes, so I was most unhappy to discover myself burned to ash and decanted into an enchanted prison."

Warwick flicked up an eyebrow. "We were surprised by your sudden death, Lord Frederick. You'd been in excellent health. Do you believe someone killed you?"

"Do you know what happened?" I asked.

"My most vivid final memories are of my coldhearted daughter-in-law standing over my bedside, telling me she wanted me gone. She deserved to rule this realm, and nothing and no one would stand in her way."

I sucked in a breath. "Lady Isolda killed you?"

"I believe she did. But I trust my son has taken her in hand for her treacherous behavior." Lord Frederick's interest returned to inspecting the room. "How fares the realm?"

Warwick inclined his head, his gaze dropping. "I'm sorry to say Lord Crosby is unwell. Lady Isolda now rules."

Lord Frederick's ashes scattered around the room and swirled around us. I covered my nose and mouth and tucked Hodgepodge's head under my armpit so he wouldn't inhale ashy, ghostly essence. No one wanted to chew on the dead.

The ghost moaned and groaned, shaking cabinets and rattling glass for several minutes before his anger subsided. He reformed, swirling angrily in front of us. "How long has this travesty been going on? I demand answers."

Warwick bowed his head fully this time. "Your son became unwell years ago. There were a few early symptoms of poor health when the dragons still supported the family, but everyone thought it would pass. It only grew worse."

Lord Frederick tilted his head. "The dragons aren't here anymore? Where have they gone? Lady Isolda rules alone?"

"It's a complicated story," I said.

Lord Frederick waved a wispy hand in the air. "Give me the briefest of summaries, but I must know what has happened in my absence."

"As your son's health declined, Lady Isolda took charge," I said. "She believed the dragons were a threat to the realm, so she trapped them in stone and turned them into a tourist attraction. Since then, she's been ruling with no one beside her."

Lord Frederick stared at me with an open mouth. "The dragons are dead? We have no dragons looking after us?"

"The realm has been without dragons for a long time," I said.

"I won't stand for this! There must be something I can do to help."

"You could convince Lady Isolda to see sense," Warwick said. "The dragons were never a threat to this realm. She made up a story about them being tainted with darkness and becoming dangerous, so she had a reason to get rid of them without anyone objecting."

He howled his disgust, and several cabinets shivered. "I have questions for that spiteful-minded creature. By removing the dragons, she has no idea what harm she has done to this realm. They protected us, ensuring order and stability."

"Things haven't been the same since Emberthorn and Stormwing were trapped," I said.

"I imagine not." Lord Frederick swirled some more. "Consider it done."

"Consider what done?" I asked.

"I'll deal with my daughter-in-law. I never intended for her to rule. I told Crosby not to marry her, but she had him bewitched. She demurred to him and pretended to respect him, but I always saw through the brittle smile into her stoney heart." Lord Frederick dispersed, leaving behind a cold wind that whipped around us for a few seconds before dying away.

"I'm not sure if we have a new ally or a new problem," I said to Warwick.

"I can't comment on Lord Frederick's ghost, but he was a decent man when alive," Warwick said. "He had old-fashioned views, but a deep respect for dragon rule."

"What's he going to do to Lady Isolda?"

Hodgepodge snuffled in my ear. "I doubt it's anything good from the way he talked about her."

There was a knock on the collection room door. Hodgepodge hid in an empty cabinet, while Warwick opened the door. A guard stood outside, and he murmured something to Warwick.

Warwick nodded. "I'll be back shortly." He left the room, leaving the other guard with me.

I returned to cleaning the silver pewter, my mind turning over what had just happened with Lord Frederick. Had Lady Isolda killed him to get her husband on the throne, and then his illness removed him from power? Or did she kill Lord Frederick, then make her husband ill so she could take over? Given what I knew about her, the last option seemed most likely.

Warwick strode back into the room and dismissed the guard. He waited until the door had closed before speaking. "There have been more reports of an assailant in the village."

"An assailant?"

"Someone is chasing people at night. Scaring them almost senseless and destroying property. I've got my soldiers looking into it. But that's the tenth report in forty-eight hours."

"Has anyone been hurt?"

"Not yet, but it's not for want of trying." Warwick gathered his things. "And you're popular. Another friend has just arrived at the gate, asking for you. I've said she can come through with her companion."

"A friend of mine? Who is it?" I asked.

"Do you know a white cat familiar named Juno?"

# Chapter 4

"This is Finn's doing. Why must he always interfere?" Hodgepodge was in the backpack as I hurried to the stable yard with Warwick shadowing me.

"He's helping! Finn said he knew the perfect people to help with our dragon situation," I whispered. "And it makes sense he'd ask Juno and Zandra to assist. After all, they helped to raise the baby dragon. They have a connection to her."

Hodgepodge grunted. "Juno is a worse show-off than Finn. And all that fluffy white fur will only draw attention. It's attention we don't need. Not when we're so close to unleashing Emberthorn and Stormwing."

"Juno will be discreet. She'll have to be."

"I doubt that snooty cat has the first idea what the word discreet means," Hodgepodge said.

"Let's find out what Finn has arranged before we make any judgments," I said. "We've got too much on our plate dealing with Stormwing's moods, Emberthorn wanting to sleep all day, and Juniper's healing. Backup is welcome. And Juno and Zandra are experts in dealing with difficult cases. Finn said so himself."

"Finn is an idiot. Juno is a show-off. And Zandra Crypt, she's not so terrible, but is easily influenced by that sassy cat. It's not natural."

Warwick listened in silence as he stayed by my side. I'd briefly filled him in on our knowledge of Juno and Zandra, which wasn't extensive, but if Finn trusted them, then so did I.

I reached into the backpack and tickled Hodgepodge's head. "Isn't that what the best familiars do? They ensure their magic users make the right decisions and help them when they get things wrong. It's not unnatural. It's the most natural of bonds. Just like the one we have."

"I still don't like them being here," Hodgepodge grumbled, but he accepted a tickle under the chin.

"The sooner we find out what their plan is, the sooner they can execute it and leave," I said. "Juniper will be of no use to us until she gets her baby back. And Stormwing won't stop stamping around and acting like the alpha dragon until she's happy. This is a win-win for all of us."

"Until Juno blasts out a flashy spell and reveals herself, taking us down with her."

"Hodgie, stop sniping. And be nice when we meet them."

Hodgepodge ducked into the backpack, still grumbling to himself.

"Keep this meeting short," Warwick said as we arrived in the stable yard. "Griffin let them into a storage shed so they wouldn't be noticed, but there are eyes and ears everywhere. Get the information you need and get out. And tell your friends not to blast magic every which way they like. I only got within five feet of that cat and my skin prickled. They need to know the rules of this realm, or they won't survive."

"Don't worry, Hodgepodge has already been telling me off about involving outsiders," I said. "We can trust them, though."

Warwick didn't look convinced, but he stood back as I headed to the storage shed where Griffin waited, his dark hair neatly clipped and his firm jaw clean shaven.

"Hey, Bell. The cat wasn't pleased about being shut in a shed," Griffin said. "She said she expected better accommodation. Although her witch friend said something about living in a basement and not to get so full of herself, so I dunno. We can trust them?"

"We can. And Juno will understand why she needs to stay out of sight when we explain how different this realm is from the world she's from. Crimson Cove has no restraints on magic."

"It has some," Zandra called out from inside the shed. "Juno, leave that alone. It's not a toy!"

"You should suggest a change of clothes for your witch friend, too. Jeans and a sweater will get her noticed. It's too modern," Griffin said.

"I'll see what I can do." I had a feeling Zandra wasn't a dress-wearing kind of woman, but we'd tackle that if we needed to.

"I'll keep watch while you're inside," Griffin said, "and let you know if there's trouble coming."

"Thanks. We appreciate it."

Griffin inched open the door, and I slid inside with Hodgepodge.

Juno was perched on Zandra's shoulder as she nonchalantly licked one white paw. She was a beautiful cat with amazing eyes, and power radiated off her in vibrant waves I'd not noticed before. The magic felt old and limitless.

Finn stepped out of the shadows and grinned. "Surprise!"

"A surprise is a whole pie fresh from the oven." Hodgepodge scrambled out of the backpack and climbed onto my shoulder. "The more people involved in this quest, the more likely it'll go wrong. You shouldn't have come back. Bell gets distracted when you're around with your big wings fluttering everywhere and those dumb dimples popping every time you smile."

"It's nice to see you too." Finn took no offence at Hodgie's rudeness. "You remember Zandra and Juno?"

I nodded. Zandra was an attractive witch, with pale skin and dark hair. Her magic felt almost as strong as Juno's, and I had to assume it was because they were a bonded pair. Witches and their familiars shared magic.

"Hodgepodge is being cautious," I said. "I'm glad you could come so quickly. Has Finn filled you in on the situation?"

"He has. Greetings," Juno said in a firm, no nonsense tone. "I understand Cinder's mother has been found."

"Cinder? That's the baby dragon's name?" I asked.

Juno nodded. "I helped to name her. How is her mother faring?"

"She's not doing good, so it'll be great to get them back together. I couldn't believe it at first when I learned her egg had been stolen." I glanced at Finn. "But it has to be a match. We worked out the timeframes, and they fit. Juniper's egg was stolen at the same time it turned up at Finn's animal sanctuary in Crimson Cove."

"I'll need to meet the dragon claiming to be Cinder's parent," Juno said. "I'm not handing her to just anyone. She's also content living in Wild Wing. The dragons have taken great care of her, although they overindulge her. She is flourishing."

"I understand your need to protect Cinder. Juniper is a good dragon, and she's pining to death over her missing baby," I said. "It would be cruel to keep them apart."

"We won't keep them apart," Zandra said. "Juno got overly attached to Cinder, though. So did Finn. Expect them to protest when the time comes to reunite mother and child. They'll be worried they won't see Cinder again."

"I'll do the right thing," Juno said. "Even if it hurts to do so."

"And I'll do my best," Finn said, "but Cinder got to me. I still hear her song in my dreams. She's one-of-a-kind. Powerful."

"She will always have that bond with us," Juno said. "We'll be there to guide her whenever she needs us."

"We wanted to help reunite them," I said, "but with everything that's going on here…"

"It's good. We know about your situation with the royal family," Zandra said. "This is some place you're living in. Rulers taking out dragons, trapping them in stone, then using them as tourist attractions. And no free use of magic? It makes my spine crawl. How do they expect people to flourish when they can't use their natural abilities?"

"They don't want us to flourish," Hodgepodge said. "Surviving is sufficient. It keeps us desperate and scared."

"I'd like a word with this royal family," Juno said. "They sound highly disrespectful. No ruler should suppress their people."

"They'll get what's coming to them," I said. "Now Emberthorn and Stormwing are free, they're healing, and we're putting a plan together to get them back on the throne."

"You focus on that. But we need an in at Wild Wing," Zandra said. "Our last visit was hectic, thanks to someone not obeying the rules."

Juno appeared unapologetic. "I did what I had to do. And everything worked out in the end."

"If you call being slung into a dragon dungeon and almost killed, sure. There was nothing to worry about." Zandra rolled her eyes, an expression of amused exasperation on her face. "Once we get access to Cinder, we can explain what's going on and figure out how to get her safely back here."

"Finally reuniting Cinder with her mother," Finn said.

"And so you don't get squashed under an angry dragon's foot because you disrespected his lady," Hodgepodge said.

"What's this?" Juno's white fur bristled, and magic sparkled over her. "Someone wants to hurt Finn?"

"Stormwing has taken a liking to Juniper," I said. "He's protective of her. And he's angry at Finn because he thinks he stole her egg and kept her apart from Cinder."

"Finn is under our protection." Juno hissed. "It could be a surly dragon or an angry magical hedgehog that has an issue with him, but they don't get to hurt him."

Finn chuckled. "It's all good, Juno. I messed up, and I've put my hands up to my mistake. Stormwing is grumpy and full of bluster, but he's behaving like that for the right reasons."

"We must move quickly on this," I said. "While Juniper still grieves, they'll all be vulnerable to attack. We need to make sure she's strong enough before we make a move on the castle. And if Stormwing is distracted because he's worrying about Juniper, this quest won't end well."

"What are you planning?" Zandra asked. "The royal family sound difficult."

"They are. But they're breaking apart, and an important wedding has diverted their attention," I said. "It's the perfect time to strike."

"Finn mentioned that, too," Juno said. "It's an ideal diversion. Weddings addle the brain."

"We hope it'll keep the family occupied while we put the final pieces in place to spring a surprise reunion with Emberthorn and Stormwing," I said.

Zandra gently nudged Juno with her head.

"Do you need our help with that too?" Juno asked. "It sounds dangerous, and I hate putting my wonderful witch in harm's way any more than I have to, but if you get stuck..."

"She does it all the time," Zandra stage-whispered.

"We don't like outsiders interfering," Hodgepodge muttered.

"We need them to interfere," I said. "Thanks for the offer. If we need extra help, can we call on you when it comes time to reveal the dragons?"

Zandra shrugged. "I've got no problem with that. We have no reason to hurry home. Things are peaceful in Crimson Cove. Barney's even taken a vacation."

"I never thought I'd see the day," Finn said. "Animal control must be quiet."

"Barney's paperwork is up to date and everyone is chilling," Zandra said. "Honestly, it's kind of dull, so I was glad to get your call."

"Cythera has been asking after you," Juno said to Finn. "She's regretting giving you so much time off."

Finn smirked. "I got it agreed in writing, so she can't go back on our arrangement. The other angels will have everything under control. And you're around if anything bad happens."

"Not at the moment," Zandra said. "Juno may be powerful, but she can't be in two places at once."

"It's possible I could. I know a spell that could arrange it." Juno twitched her whiskers. "But it would be draining. And we need our attention on these dragons. I'm looking forward to going back to Wild Wing."

"Just make sure you don't get thrown into the dragon dungeon pit," Finn said.

Hodgepodge hissed. "It'll happen again if you blast your magic about as if you have an endless supply and don't care who it strikes."

"Well... I wouldn't say endless," Juno said. "But I suspect I have significantly more power than you."

"I doubt she can go super-size like you can," I whispered to Hodgepodge.

He grumbled but seemed calmed by my comment.

"Be careful about using magic freely," I said. "This realm has fierce restrictions on the type of spells that can be used. If a royal guard sees you casting an unauthorized spell, it'll be straight to the dungeon."

"The guards don't concern me," Juno said.

"They should," Finn said. "This place is full of magic users who are prevented from using their powers. Barely anyone is spared. Since I arrived, I've been followed to see what magic I'm using, so I've been keeping things quiet."

"That's the vibe I've felt ever since we got here," Zandra said. "It feels like a cauldron is about to bubble over. All this repressed magic that's desperate to blast out."

"Let's hope it blasts in the direction of the royal family," Hodgepodge said.

"We'll keep things on the down low," Zandra said. "Don't worry about us messing up."

"I'll get word to Wild Wing today and make an appointment for you to see the dragons," I said. "Once they know the situation, they'll be eager to unite Cinder and Juniper. Dragons thrive when they're with their biological family."

"We did a magnificent job raising Cinder." Juno's fur bristled. "She grew wonderfully big and strong under our care."

"I'm sure she did," I said as pragmatically as possible. "But it's the dragon magic that's so important when raising an infant. It's unique to mother and child. If the young one isn't exposed to it, it can cause behavioral issues."

Zandra chuckled. "We know all about that. We were always putting out fires when that baby got in a grump or didn't get her own way. And she wouldn't leave Juno's ears alone, no matter how many times she was put on the naughty mat in Vorana's kitchen."

"Cinder could be overexcitable." Juno fussed with an ear. "We knew what we were doing. We read every book in Vorana's bookstore. We're dragon rearing experts."

"Maybe don't brag about that when you meet the dragons in Wild Wing," I said. "Be respectful and expect them to put up resistance. And they'll want all the information before they're willing to let Cinder go."

"I'll tell them everything about my involvement and accept any punishment they feel is suitable." Finn's wings drooped.

"I won't allow any punishment. You did nothing wrong," Juno said.

"Maybe I deserve it. I should never have kept Juniper's egg. But I got so busy, and then with the dragon song... I had no option but to protect Cinder."

"The dragons should focus on who stole the egg," Zandra said. "They're the criminals. You were only trying to help."

As Finn, Juno, and Zandra discussed a suitable punishment, I wondered if I should go to Wild Wing with them. I sensed tension brewing as Juno and Zandra defended Finn's actions. Dragons were quick to offend, and we didn't need disharmony at such an important time.

The storage shed door inched open, and Warwick peered in. "Are you done? There's something going on inside the castle. I'm needed."

"We should get out of here. Is there a back way out?" Zandra asked. "People looked at me funny as we walked through the market."

"It's your modern clothing," I said. "We're traditional around here."

"Don't expect me to wear one of those dresses." Zandra gestured at me. "You look like a medieval tavern wench."

"My skirt is practical! It has pockets." I demonstrated by flaring the fabric.

"You always look splendid in a dress," Juno said to Zandra. She lifted a paw. "I can whisk you up something suitable."

"No skirt! I'll be tripping over it all the time."

"Maybe try a cloak?" I suggested. "It'll provoke less curiosity if you cover what you're wearing."

"I'll see what I can find in the market. Use this to keep in touch with us." Zandra handed me a palm-sized rectangular object with small crystal-like orbs dancing inside it.

I turned it over. "What does it do?"

"It's a mobile snow globe. We use them to send messages and call each other. It's the easiest way to stay in touch. Especially if you're not supposed to use magic."

"I've heard of these devices, but they're forbidden around here," I said. "Even when the dragons ruled, the family was strict on the type of magical technology available to us."

"Then your royal family are jerks," Zandra said. "I'll be in touch on that. You do likewise."

I slipped it into a skirt pocket. "Got it. And thanks for helping."

We said our goodbyes, and Griffin ushered Juno, Zandra, and Finn out of the shed.

I stepped into the courtyard and froze. Guards dashed in and out of the castle, and a group of people stood together, looking worried as they kept glancing at the frantic activity.

I dashed over to them. "What's going on?"

"Something happened to Prince Jasper," an elderly man said. "He's been attacked."

My thoughts turned to Camilla and her murder list. "Did you see what happened?"

"No, they've shut the main door and aren't letting anyone other than guards inside."

I hurried away with Hodgepodge toward the servants' entrance. Fortunately, the way was open, and I entered without being stopped.

"Do you think Camilla has finally acted on her desire to get rid of Prince Jasper?" Hodgepodge whispered.

"She wants him dead," I said. "And when we last saw her, she had me worried. There was a look in her eyes I didn't trust."

"I've never trusted Camilla," Hodgepodge said. "If it was her, let's hope they caught her in the act. That'll get her out of our hair."

"Hodgie! She'll get taken to the castle dungeon, and her life will be over. We wouldn't wish that on our worst enemy."

"Better her than us."

I raced along the corridor and took the exit that led into the main castle hallway. There was a crowd gathered at the foot of the stairs, the air tense with nervous anxiety and fear. And there was a strange smell. One I couldn't place.

A haze of magic flickered by the stairs, and Seraphina blinked into view, her arms full of potions. She parted the crowd and disappeared as she crouched.

"Where is he?" Lady Isolda appeared at the top of the stairs and swept down them, surrounded by her assistants. "Get out of my way, idiots. I must see my son."

The crowd parted again, finally giving us a proper glimpse of Prince Jasper.

My breath caught, and I clutched Hodgepodge. Prince Jasper lay on his back, a blade sticking out of him.

# Chapter 5

We stayed out of sight, as shocked onlookers watched Seraphina tend to Prince Jasper's injuries. From this distance, I couldn't tell if he was alive, but by the feverish way Seraphina cast spells and poured potions, I had to assume she was confident in bringing him back.

Lady Isolda blasted out a spell, sending the onlookers scattering. "If you can't be useful, leave. And if anyone is still here the next time I look up, consider your names added to my death list."

"She has a death list?" Hodgepodge whispered.

"Nothing would surprise me about Lady Isolda," I replied. "Can you tell if Prince Jasper is breathing?"

"No, but I don't see any blood. Maybe the knife didn't go in too deeply."

"Seraphina will save him," I said. "She's allowed to use unlimited types of magic."

"She's been pushing herself hard with Emberthorn and Stormwing. Now she has Juniper to heal as well, it's draining her power. She may not be able to save him."

"I thought you were happy Seraphina was working herself to death. Suitable punishment for betraying the dragons." My gaze remained glued to the scene as people hurried away to avoid Lady Isolda's sharp gaze and even sharper magic.

"She's paid for her misdeeds. And the way her hands are shaking, she'll be no use to anyone if she refuses to take care of herself."

"Lady Isolda doesn't care about that," I said. "She won't lose her only son. If Prince Jasper dies, that's it for the Ithric family line."

"If he doesn't make it, she'll pry mad Lord Crosby from his turret and insist he does his husbandly duty so she produces another heir."

I grimaced. "Lady Isolda is powerful, but even she can't undo the destruction caused when the dragons were taken. She won't be able to sire another child until they're back."

"And even their return may not fix the mess this family has made of things." Hodgepodge stilled, and his eyes narrowed. "Prince Jasper's feet twitched."

It was easier to see now the crowd had departed. The only people left in the hallway were Lady Isolda, Seraphina, and a dozen guards. Warwick was among them. Every few minutes, a guard would appear and report back to him then be dismissed.

"They're looking for Prince Jasper's attacker," I whispered.

"I hope whoever did it got out. If they know about the servants' tunnels, they could have escaped, even with the main doors bolted."

"I don't think Camilla knows about the tunnels. She's got to be the prime suspect." I chewed on my bottom lip. "Stabbing was on her list of ways to kill him. Where is she? She must have heard the commotion. Not being around makes her look guilty."

"She most likely is guilty. Camilla probably snapped as the wedding slithered ever closer and she ran out of excuses to avoid Prince Jasper's bed. He must have said or done something to push her over the edge. The first chance she got, she used a blade on him."

"Why do it in such a public place? If Camilla wanted to kill Prince Jasper, she could have lured him into his chambers, pretending she wanted to seduce him. He'd have been willing to go with her. Once they were behind closed doors, she could have attacked without interruption."

"Camilla's not of sound mind or judgment. Maybe Prince Jasper insulted her, she chased him, and grabbed the first weapon that came to hand," Hodgepodge said.

"And now she's in hiding," I said. "The way Warwick is ordering the guards around, she won't stay hidden for long. They'll search every inch of this castle until they discover her."

Seraphina looked up at Lady Isolda and spoke a few words. Whatever they were, Lady Isolda seemed slightly less furious, and the magic flickering off her fingertips faded.

"Move him," Lady Isolda snapped.

Seraphina unrolled a plain gray strip of fabric, ran her hand over it, and it lifted into the air. Two guards moved Prince Jasper onto the floating gurney and assisted Seraphina in taking him up the stairs.

"Seraphina has worked her magic," Hodgepodge said. "She's had enough practice on the dragons to heal just about anyone from any injury."

Lady Isolda stood with her hands on her hips for several minutes, looking around the vast expanse of cold grey hallway. She gestured Warwick over. They talked for several minutes, Lady Isolda's sentences becoming shorter, her gestures more frantic.

"Warwick needs to be careful," Hodgepodge muttered. "He may be Lady Isolda's right-hand man, but she'll be quick to strike him down if he fails in this mission."

Another minute passed, and Warwick assembled a team of twelve guards, and they marched our way. I ducked out of sight.

"She was last seen on the upper levels," Warwick said. "We split into four teams and search every room. As soon as we find Camilla, we'll bring her to Lady Isolda. If you value your life, don't deviate from that order. No matter how hard Camilla protests, she must be taken to Lady Isolda as soon as possible."

We waited until the guards passed before relaxing.

"What a surprise," Hodgepodge hissed softly. "Lady Isolda has been looking for a reason to get rid of Camilla."

"Maybe Lady Isolda stabbed her own son in the back," I said. "She can blame the attack on Camilla and get rid of a problem."

"She'd be cruel enough to do it," Hodgepodge said.

"We should help Camilla. She may not know how much trouble is coming her way."

"We stay out of this, lassie," Hodgepodge said. "There's no point getting caught up in any more complications. We'll find ourselves in the dungeon and won't be able to help Emberthorn and Stormwing from there."

"Camilla has been through so much since she arrived," I said. "If Lady Isolda is framing her for trying to murder Prince Jasper, we must warn her. We can give her enough time to flee with her sister so they can return to their family."

"And be followed by war! That's what Lady Isolda will bring down on their heads for breaking a deal and trying to murder a member of her family. We don't need this problem. We already have enough."

"It doesn't have to be a problem." I followed the guards at a discreet distance. "All we have to do is tell Camilla she's in trouble. She can decide what to do next. Maybe she'll want to face Lady Isolda and prove she's innocent."

"When Camilla learns what's happened, she'll laugh in your face and tell you it's the best news she's heard all day. Then she'll produce a knife and stab you as well." Hodgepodge flared his neck ruff.

"Camilla is eccentric and takes too many risks, but I've never felt unsafe around her. If the roles were reversed, I'd want someone to warn me if trouble was coming my way."

Hodgepodge huffed out a breath. "If we're doing this foolish thing, we'll need magic to conceal us. Warwick is leading the guards to the stairs, so they're planning a top-down search. We won't be able to get to the family level without questions being asked."

I flexed my hands. My magic felt powerful, and I was certain I could cloak us so no one would see us as we moved through the castle.

Hodgepodge sighed. "Let's get this over with. But I want a reward afterward. Something sweet. Pie. A whole one to myself."

"If we get out of this alive, you can have as much pie as you like." I ducked into a quiet corridor, spread my hands, and cast a spell. Magic tingled over my skin, and a few seconds later, we were invisible. It was almost as easy as breathing.

I hurried after the guards as they headed up the stairs to the family rooms. They split off into four groups, and I followed Warwick. I hoped he'd find Camilla. He'd have to take her to Lady Isolda, but he wouldn't be cruel about it. Some of the guards had a mean streak and were overly fond of using those sparking sticks they carried.

We dashed past expensive oil paintings, giant wall tapestries, and priceless antiques in the corridor. The guards swiftly searched each room, and I breathed a sigh of relief every time they came out empty-handed.

Warwick stopped by the entrance to Grand Dame Ravenswood's prison turret. "I'll lead us up. At the first sign of trouble, everyone retreats. Her last bad mood put two of you in the hospital for a week."

His guards exchanged worried glances but nodded before thumping their staffs on the floor and activating the magic.

Warwick unbound the powerful magic laced around the door, tearing it off with his hands as he muttered an unlock spell. It took several minutes before the way was clear. It was a testament to just how strong Grand Dame Ravenswood's magic was.

He inched open the door and peered inside then gestured for the guards to follow. We were right on their heels and joined them in climbing the circular stone staircase. Several times, Warwick stopped and unbound more magic before we could go farther.

"I have a bad feeling about this," Hodgepodge whispered. "If you need to trap someone in so much magic, they can't be fun to spend time with."

"I remember Grand Dame Ravenswood when she was free to walk around the castle. She was quirky even then, but she had such a thirst for life. She used to come into the kitchen and talk to Alice about food. No one really knows what happened to get her trapped up here."

"Her spiteful family happened. She wouldn't play by their rules, so she had her freedom taken," Hodgepodge said.

A guard turned and peered down the stairs, putting an end to our mutterings.

We reached the top of the turret. Warwick knocked on the door and waited. It took several minutes and a few more knocks, but the door creaked open. There was no one on the other side.

"Grand Dame Ravenswood," Warwick said. "It's Warwick Woodsbane. Do I have your permission to enter?"

"Warwick! Of course. You're always welcome, unless you're here to issue another decree of restriction from that viper who sits on the throne and pretends she knows how to rule." Grand Dame Ravenswood's voice was a smoky warble with a deep undertone of determined, no nonsense grit.

Warwick entered first, and the guards remained by the entrance, so we had no option but to lurk behind them.

"Don't cower in my doorway. You may all enter," she said. "Unless you're afraid. Have the vicious whispers and rumors spread about me set your guards shaking in fear, Warwick?"

Under Warwick's instruction, the guards inched inside, allowing us to enter, too. I tiptoed to a corner by the door and breathed as quietly as possible. They left the door open. Most likely, so Warwick and his guards could make a quick escape if they had to.

The turret was a vast space, constructed of pale sandstone bricks. There were sumptuous rugs underfoot, tapestries on every wall, and the furnishings looked luxurious and were covered in furs that I hoped were fake.

Grand Dame Ravenswood reclined on a large, comfortable looking couch, dressed head to toe in black with a startling array of red and black feathers stuck in her hair. That hair was a glorious deep russet that hung to her waist and must have been tinged with magic. Her face was remarkably unlined for a woman of such advanced years, which suggested she used magic not only on her hair but on her appearance.

And this stunning vision of enchanted nobility wasn't alone. Camilla sat on the couch opposite her.

"My apologies for interrupting," Warwick said, "but I've been sent to collect Miss Oldsbrook. Lady Isolda has need of her."

Grand Dame Ravenswood lifted her chin an inch, her gaze as icy as her daughter-in-law's as she regarded Warwick. "*I* have need of her. She is visiting me. Tell that cold creature to wait her turn."

"You may not be aware, but there has been an incident concerning Prince Jasper," Warwick said.

"Has he gotten drunk again?" Camilla asked. "He starts drinking earlier every day. Nothing I say will dissuade him from picking up a decanter. How can he expect to receive my affections when he behaves in such a slovenly manner?"

"Prince Jasper has been injured," Warwick said. "Lady Isolda is concerned Miss Oldsbrook may have been involved in the attack."

"Attack!" Grand Dame Ravenswood sat up straight. "When did this alleged attack happen? Where?"

"Inside the castle. Someone stabbed Prince Jasper in the back," Warwick said. "Miss Oldsbrook, please come with me. Lady Isolda is waiting."

Camilla gasped then laughed. "Someone finally got to him. It's about time. Hateful little man."

The guards shifted from foot to foot until a glare from Warwick stilled them.

"You're wasting your time coming here," Grand Dame Ravenswood said. "Camilla has been with me for the past hour. I'm assuming my grandson was only recently stabbed?"

"He was found ten minutes ago in the castle atrium," Warwick said.

"Then leave us. It couldn't have been Camilla. We've been here discussing her wedding and all the fuss and fancy being forced upon the poor creature."

The guards behind Warwick stepped forward. With a flick of her hand, Grand Dame Ravenswood knocked them off their feet and slammed them into the wall, making them drop their staffs.

"Go. Leave us. That's my final word on this matter. Collect your guards and remove yourself from my space, unless you want me to see if you'll fit out of the turret window." Grand Dame Ravenswood wiggled her fingers at Warwick, a vicious smile crusting her lips.

"I should have known she'd be hiding up here with you." Lady Isolda appeared in the doorway, sparking with fury.

"You aren't welcome in my domain." Grand Dame Ravenswood stood slowly, uncoiling like a snake preparing for an attack, her gaze fixed on Lady Isolda.

"You had to get your claws into her and poison her already damaged mind." Lady Isolda didn't move from the doorway. Was she also afraid of Grand Dame Ravenswood?

"You're doing a perfect job of that yourself," Grand Dame Ravenswood said. "Camilla has told me everything. It's no wonder she doesn't want to marry into this family. And I've informed her of your twisted treatment of me and how evil you are. She has assured me I'll be released once she's married."

"There won't be a marriage if Jasper doesn't survive," Lady Isolda said. "And he's injured because of Camilla's irrational act!"

"It couldn't have happened to a nicer grandson." Grand Dame Ravenswood smirked. "Well, I can think of one other grandson who deserves to be stabbed in the back, but he's trying his hand in conquering the treacherous waters that surround us. I hope a great white porpoise has eaten him. How is Godric? Have you heard word of his adventures, or did he forget you the second he left the castle?"

"Keep your insane prattling to yourself," Lady Isolda snarled. "Camilla, come with me."

"You do not get to order her around." Grand Dame Ravenswood swooped in front of Lady Isolda, defying her aged bones with the swift movement. "I've already told Warwick that Camilla was with me when Jasper was stabbed. Now, go away before I test my magic and see if it'll blow your head clean off those bony shoulders."

"You cannot speak to me like that," Lady Isolda hissed.

"I'm your elder and by far your better, so I may speak to you in any way I desire. Take your mewling lapdogs and leave."

The alpha females stared at each other, magic flickering between them, the air sparking with their mutual desire to destroy.

Lady Isolda surprised me by being the first to break eye contact. "Camilla, come to my rooms as soon as you are available. You will not be able to leave the castle, so make no attempt to escape. If you do, I'll assume you had a hand in stabbing my son."

Camilla no longer smiled, seeming to understand the seriousness of the situation. She nodded.

Lady Isolda turned and marched out of the door, gesturing for the guards to follow. We remained in place, still concealed under a veil of magic, stunned by what we'd seen and overheard.

If Camilla hadn't stabbed Prince Jasper in the back, then who had?

# Chapter 6

Hodgepodge was stretched out, so he was full length, resting his head on my chest, his tail hanging down by my knees. "Every day should be like this. No starting work as the sun comes up and you having to chip ice off the water to wash. No running through frozen streets for fear of being late and angering Lady Isolda. Just warmth, blankets, good food, and you to lie on."

My smile felt lazy as I rested a hand on his head. "I'm still getting used to not having to get up to start work at dawn. I'm waking at the same time, but at least now we get to lounge in our favorite chair before getting going."

My work in the family's private collection room had taken some adjusting. I didn't enjoy being under constant guard, but provided that guard was Warwick, I couldn't object. I even tentatively considered him a friend. An immensely grumpy friend, but he counted.

Overall, life felt better. My wage was still terrible, and my lodgings had no heating other than the open fire, but this change in work pattern gave me more time with the dragons and an occasional snuggle with Hodgepodge. It was a beneficial side-effect of helping Emberthorn and Stormwing escape the stone chamber and one I was certain the family wouldn't have bestowed upon me if they knew of my involvement in breaking them out.

"We'll have ten more minutes before we have to leave, then we must move off this seat," I said.

"We've got ages." Hodgepodge rolled on to his back so I could tickle his belly.

"We need to get to the castle to find out how Prince Jasper is doing. He may not have made it through the night." I scratched my nails gently across Hodgepodge's scales.

"Seraphina will have saved him. If he'd been critical, Lady Isolda wouldn't have sent him up to his room like a misbehaving schoolboy."

"Maybe he was already dead, but she didn't want to panic anyone. The second word gets out he's gone, all hope will be lost that there'll ever be a new royal heir."

"Lady Isolda doesn't care about anyone else's reaction," Hodgepodge said. "She seemed more interested in finding out who did it."

"Or figuring out how to pin the blame on Camilla."

"Don't feel too sorry for Camilla. She's dragged us too close to danger to want to keep her as a friend," Hodgepodge said.

"I don't like her being used as a pawn in the Ithric games. All she wants to do is help her family out of a difficult situation, but she's not safe here."

"Neither will we be if we poke our noses into things that don't concern us. We stick with the dragons. Camilla will have to fend for herself. And she's not alone anymore. Not now Valerie is here to help with the wedding."

I softly sighed. "I do need to focus on Emberthorn, Stormwing, and Juniper. I still find it hard to believe we have three dragons in hiding."

"And will soon have a fourth if Juno, Zandra, and Finn don't make a mess of their mission. Why haven't they been in touch?"

I slid the mobile snow globe from my skirt pocket and turned it over several times.

Hodgepodge jabbed his nose against it several times, causing the glowing flakes inside to lift. "Be careful who you show that to."

"It'll stay buried in my pocket. I'm uncertain how to use it, but I suppose it's simple enough. I'll wait for them to send a message and then work out how to reply."

Hodgepodge jabbed his nose against it again and made it beep, causing him to rear back and hiss. "If you get caught with that thing, you'll be in trouble."

"We need a way to communicate with everyone," I said.

"They should have used the enchanted owl network," Hodgepodge said.

"Those poor owls are so antiquated they fly as badly as the dragons when they escaped the castle, and they're always delivering messages to the wrong houses. Barely anyone uses them anymore." I turned the device over again. It had gone dark. I hoped it hadn't been damaged by Hodgepodge poking at it. I slid it back into my pocket. "Finn is always using his globe to stay in touch with people."

"Then I know it can't be used for doing good." Hodgepodge poked out his tongue at the mention of my new angel friend. "He probably sends summons to his demon buddies."

"You need to be nicer to Finn. He's not going anywhere."

"He can't stay forever. He has a home of his own and a job in Crimson Cove. That's a long way from here."

I sighed. I enjoyed Finn's company, but I needed to be prepared for when he left. As nice as it was having him in the village, I couldn't expect him to uproot things so we could spend more time together. We were friends. Nothing more. But I loved that smile of his.

Hodgepodge nipped my chin. "Don't get all googly-eyed over that angel-demon. We have a mission to focus on. Well, two missions. The dragons and making sure I have an endless supply of delicious, sweet pie."

"I haven't forgotten about my pie promise. I'll grab some from the market during our lunch break."

Hodgepodge slid me a glare. "Will we be eating alone? Or will that pesky angel-demon put in an appearance?"

"Finn can do as he pleases. I haven't invited him to lunch." I kissed Hodgepodge on the head. "Since you talk about him so much, maybe you'd like me to extend an invitation."

Hodgepodge huffed out a plume of smoke. "He's too free with his magic. So were Juno and Zandra when they arrived. And that cat is too powerful. No single creature should feel so strong. Everyone will sense it."

I rested my head back against the soft seat. "We used to be like that. It's getting harder to remember a time when we used magic without looking over our shoulders. I miss those days. Once Emberthorn and Stormwing are back, things will change for the better."

"They won't change at all if we don't get them focused on taking back control and not obsessing over Cinder."

"While we're lounging here, we won't make progress with any of our tasks." I stood and hefted Hodgepodge onto my shoulder. "Let's see how Seraphina is doing."

I locked my door and walked along the busy street, people dashing back and forth and calling out greetings. The main castle doors were open, but there were double the usual number of guards outside. Lady Isolda was taking no chances. That meant they hadn't found who'd stabbed Prince Jasper, or she hadn't made up enough evidence to frame Camilla for the crime, so she needed to appear concerned for everyone's safety.

"Let's enter through the servants' entrance," I whispered to Hodgepodge, who was once again in the backpack I carried, so he had a safe place to hide.

He grunted his approval, so I sidled past the gate, around the side of the castle, and through the small door cut into the thick stone wall. The corridor was cool and slightly damp as I dashed along.

I entered the main hallway and walked to Seraphina's private rooms. She had expansive quarters, made to house the reference books and lore she'd collected over the years, but she also conducted experiments using magic under the orders of the royal family. That meant she needed room to store potions, charms, and spells.

I knocked on her door and waited a moment. The bolt on the other side finally slid back, and Seraphina peered at me through the gap. She opened the door wider when she saw it was me and ushered me in before locking the door.

"Did you get to the forest last night?" I asked. "Or were you too busy looking after Prince Jasper?"

"The family took my complete attention yesterday," she said with a weary sigh. "The dragons will be fine, though. I sent Evander and Astrid with the potions they needed to continue their healing."

"And Prince Jasper? I saw him after he got stabbed. He didn't look so good." I followed her to our usual seating area close to the book stacks, the smell of book dust and strong tea, ever present scents.

Seraphina sank into a chair. "He survived. The knife hit nothing vital, and after running tests, I discovered the blade wasn't enchanted with anything nasty. He got lucky. He's in his rooms, complaining bitterly that he's not allowed to lie on his back."

I sat in a chair opposite her, and Hodgepodge climbed out of the backpack and hurried to the kitchen to see if there were any scraps he could salvage. "Does Prince Jasper know who did it?"

"He didn't see a thing. Whoever it was crept up from behind and stabbed him. All he remembers is a hot pain in his back, and then he was shoved. He recalls footsteps running away, but that's it."

"Is Lady Isolda questioning anyone?"

"The way she's ranting, she thinks everyone in the castle is guilty of something." Seraphina pinched the bridge of her nose.

"I followed Warwick and his guards after the incident to see what they would uncover. I overheard them talking. Camilla is in trouble."

"You can never keep out of a mystery, can you, Bell?" Seraphina's smile was tired as she scratched the back of her hand. "When I was with Prince Jasper, all Lady Isolda kept asking him was if it was Camilla. Did he recognize her footsteps, her perfume, or hear her laugh? But he's not convinced it was her."

"Then Prince Jasper underestimates his fiancée," I said. "It's all she talks about when she's with me."

"Lady Isolda is determined to pin this on Camilla, no matter what it takes," Seraphina said. "But no witnesses have come forward to say they saw her stalking Prince Jasper, so Lady Isolda's hands are tied."

"It wasn't Camilla," I said. "Warwick visited Grand Dame Ravenswood's turret, and Camilla was there."

"I heard the same thing," Seraphina said. "I'm concerned Lady Isolda may still find a way to implicate Camilla. They despise each other."

"If no one saw anything, there's little she can do to make Camilla appear guilty," I said.

"Lady Isolda is worried, but I see cunning in her eyes. She's convincing everyone the attacker could strike again and is claiming someone wants to stop the wedding and ensure no royal heir is born."

"There won't be a royal heir, anyway." Hodgepodge returned from the kitchen, chewing on something. "No matter how physically perfect Camilla is, she can't break the curse that hangs over this realm. Only the dragons' return will do that."

"Every test I've run on Camilla shows she's exactly what we need. She could safely deliver a baby every year for the next ten years and be unfazed."

"Camilla's not the problem, though, is she?" I said.

"Are you going to tell the Ithric family that?" Seraphina shook her head.

"Do you think Lady Isolda has a right to be worried about another attack?" I asked.

"If someone wants this wedding stopped, they could try again and take out either Prince Jasper or Camilla," Seraphina said.

I sat forward in my seat, worry trickling through me. "Maybe the attack doesn't have to do with stopping the wedding because they want the family to fail. Prince Jasper was attacked because someone knows how miserable Camilla will be when they marry. They've learned how desperately unhappy she is and how unkind Prince Jasper is to her."

Hodgepodge jumped onto my lap. "We should talk to her sister, Valerie."

# Chapter 7

As promised, I took Hodgepodge to the pie stall during our lunch break and bought delicious slices of cherry pie with a sugar-crusted pastry top. As much as I wanted to linger over the pie, I had another mission in mind. Ever since I'd talked to Seraphina about the motives for wanting Prince Jasper dead, I needed to find Valerie and see what she knew about the attack.

"Have we got time for a second slice?" Hodgepodge asked as I licked sugar from my fingertips.

"No more pie for you. Too much fruit upsets your tummy."

"I can handle another slice. I'm a growing wyvern. Now I go super-size all the time, I burn extra calories. Pie has loads of calories."

"Then wait until you're giant before you gorge on pie again." I stood, cleared our outside dining table, and then lifted the backpack with Hodgepodge in. I walked through the busy market, sellers shouting about various goodies to tempt passersby, and headed inside the castle, using the servants' tunnel and going straight to the stone chamber.

When I arrived, it was still a hectic haze of wedding paraphernalia, but I was surprised to find Griffin there. This time of day, he was usually in the stables with the horses. But he was helping Valerie, carrying a pile of wrapped gifts carefully balanced between his arm and hip. Valerie also carried a mass of gifts, although she struggled with hers.

I dashed over before she dropped a parcel. "Can I help?"

Valerie smiled when she saw me. "Thanks. Can you believe how many wedding presents are already arriving?"

"It's people currying favor with the new royal couple," Griffin said. "I keep getting disturbed in the yard with deliveries when people get lost and don't know where to offload the gifts."

I grabbed several more wrapped packages from Valerie's load to help her.

"We're putting them on the table on the far side of the room. I haven't been told if the happy couple wants to open them now or after the big day, so I'm storing them out of the way, so no one trips over them." Valerie adjusted her load.

"They have other things to worry about." Griffin set down his packages and took the rest of Valerie's parcels.

"You've heard what happened yesterday?" I asked.

"Of course. Who hasn't? But it's not just that I'm thinking about. There have been more attacks in the village," Griffin said.

My brow furrowed. "Warwick mentioned something about that. People being chased?"

"No one knows who it is, but there's a thing hiding in the shadows and jumping out at people."

"A thing? Not a person?" I asked.

"Apparently, the creature, or whatever it is, growls and roars before chasing anyone. People flee in terror. I've heard rumors it was made with dark magic."

"Has anyone been hurt?"

Griffin shook his head. "Not yet, but whatever manner of monster it is, it'll get lucky eventually."

Valerie shuddered. "The streets sound dangerous."

"I'll walk you anywhere you need to go," Griffin said. "It'll be no trouble."

I smiled at his chivalry. "If you ever get into trouble, Griffin is handy with a blade. He used to be a royal guard."

Valerie's cheeks flushed. "I may take you up on that offer. What with a shadowy attacker prowling and what happened to Prince Jasper, the whole place feels unstable. Everyone is gossiping about the stabbing. I'm still in shock it happened inside the castle walls. With all these soldiers around, you'd think nothing like that could happen."

"I'll watch out for you." There was a protective note in Griffin's voice. "They'll have to come through me before they get inside this chamber."

Valerie ducked her head. "That's sweet of you. You've been sweet all day, dealing with the gifts and that awful man who came here earlier."

"What happened?" I asked.

"Some jerk was throwing his weight around, telling Valerie what to do, like she was a common servant. I put him in his place," Griffin said.

I smiled to myself. Griffin liked Valerie, and I hoped he had the courage to do something about these newfound feelings. He always felt people considered him valueless since he lost his arm, but he was one of the most valuable and loyal friends I had. The battles we'd faced together convinced me I'd be happy to have him defending my back in times of trouble.

"I'm glad you're being looked after so well," I said to Valerie. "How's Camilla?"

Valerie glanced around to make sure we weren't being overheard. "I'm worried about her. Since she's been here, she's changed."

"I haven't known Camilla for long, but I've noticed she can be impulsive," I said. "Is that what's different about her since she moved to the castle?"

"No. Camilla was always what our parents called quirky, but I've never seen her so... elsewhere. She's always had these flights of fancy and would disappear into a dreamworld. I'd tell her to write down her imaginings, but she never had the discipline for that," Valerie said. "She'd tell me them, though."

"There's nothing wrong with a healthy imagination," I said.

"I don't disagree. But since she moved here, Camilla's spending more time in her fantasy worlds. She told me it's the only way she can cope with staying here." Valerie chewed on her thumbnail.

"It takes some adjusting to live here," I said. "Nearly every other realm, town, or village has fewer rules about magic. And, of course, many still have their dragons looking after them."

"It's more than that. Although it is strange to be in a place where you always feel like you're being watched," Valerie said. "I asked a guard yesterday if it was okay to use a certain spell. It was nothing special, but he said I couldn't cast it and told me not to use any magic in case I got in trouble."

"It's how we all live," Griffin said. "It's not enjoyable, but you must toe the line for now. You don't want to come to the attention of Lady Isolda's guards. Being Camilla's sister won't keep you safe."

"I stay far away from them," Valerie said. "They're intimidating. I suppose they're meant to be, but it's different from back home. Our soldiers keep us safe, not terrify us into obedience."

"Camilla must be struggling with that aspect of life here, too," I said.

"I fear so. But as hard as it is for her, our family needs this marriage to work. I'd take Camilla's place if I could, but that's not an option." Valerie lifted a hand to her crooked back.

"Anyone would be grateful to have you as their wife," Griffin said. "You're kind, intelligent, loyal to your family. And you have the prettiest smile I've ever seen."

Hodgepodge snort-laughed from inside my backpack, making Griffin blush.

"It's good you'd be willing to make the sacrifice and marry into this family," I said to Valerie to distract from Griffin's pink cheeks. "But is such a sacrifice really worth it?"

"To ensure our family's prosperity? Absolutely. Not all realms thrive. A difficult war on the border has troubled ours for almost a decade. We have two dragons who support us, but they're elderly and stuck in their ways. They resist change. They do their best, but the realm suffers. This partnership between Camilla and Prince Jasper gives us access to more trade routes. Money will return, and we will thrive again. We'll be able to fund the war and put an end to so much misery."

"I heard there were last-minute changes to the deal, though," I said.

"Camilla has been telling you all our secrets!" Valerie blinked at me with surprise in her eyes.

"Bell is easy to talk to," Griffin said. "You can rely on her to do the right thing. And she doesn't gossip."

"That's good of you to say." I smiled warmly at Griffin. "I listened to Camilla when she was lonely and needed a friendly face. Someone to talk to when Prince Jasper didn't turn out to be quite the charming prince everyone thought he was."

Valerie was silent for a moment, her gaze on the wedding preparations. "It's true. The Ithric family renegotiated terms. We still get access to the trade routes, but they're heavily taxed. We can't afford not to take the deal, though. It will help. It has to."

"At least you're here now to help ease Camilla into this new way of living." I wanted to share that it wouldn't be like this for much longer, but the fewer people who knew about Emberthorn and Stormwing being free, the better.

"I wanted to be here sooner to help Camilla get used to the changes, but our parents struggle when we're both gone. And Lady Isolda was slow to extend an invitation to any of us. But she couldn't keep me from my own sister's wedding."

"What if your family found another way to fund the war?" I asked. "You could get Camilla out of this unhappy marriage. Put a stop to her misery."

Valerie was quiet, her attention on the wrapped gifts. "Sometimes, sacrifices must be made. We were born into this life, so we know what's expected of us. Well, what's expected of Camilla. I'll remain helpful to my parents as they age. That's the best I can hope for."

Griffin inhaled as if to say something of importance but stopped himself and adjusted the gifts on the table.

"I noticed more guards around than usual," I said. "The family must be worried the attacker could strike again."

"If they did, and we lost Prince Jasper, would that be a bad thing?" Griffin asked.

"It would for my family," Valerie said. "No wedding means the deal falls apart. Camilla would have to return home in disgrace. We'd be left with nothing. We'd lose the war. My family would be captured and sent to prison. Prince Jasper must survive!"

Valerie's sincerity and concern for her family gave me pause about her guilt. She loved Camilla, and wanted to protect her, but she needed to look after all of her family and consider the safety of her homeland. Stabbing Prince Jasper put everything they'd worked for at risk.

"Has Lady Isolda spoken to you about what happened to Prince Jasper?" I asked. "I was there just after he was found, and she's determined to discover who attacked her son."

Valerie grimaced. "She spoke to me. Well, she spoke *at* me. She insisted I hide nothing and kept telling me not to cover for Camilla and just because we were family didn't mean I should hide the truth."

I lifted my eyebrows. "The truth about what?"

Valerie leaned in close. "I'm concerned she's implicating Camilla in the stabbing."

"Why? This marriage benefits the Ithric family, too," Griffin said. "Camilla was picked because she's a perfect match for Prince Jasper. She's guaranteed to give him a royal heir."

"What if Lady Isolda is having doubts?" I asked. "Camilla has been feisty since she moved here. Lady Isolda isn't used to being spoken back to or disobeyed."

"You think she's tiring of Camilla?" Valerie's eyes widened.

"It's possible. Until we figure out who attacked Prince Jasper, I'm concerned you and Camilla are vulnerable."

"Bell, can I have a word in private?" Griffin caught hold of my elbow and propelled me away from Valerie before I could reply. "What are you doing?"

"Looking for answers. Lady Isolda is after Camilla for the stabbing. If Camilla hadn't been with Grand Dame Ravenswood when it took place, she'd have been executed by now."

"But terrifying Valerie by telling her that does no good," Griffin said. "What do you expect her to do about this mess?"

I glanced at Valerie, who was watching us talk. "I wondered if she was behind the attack."

"Bell!"

"Wait. Having spoken to her, I don't think she'd risk ruining the deal made. It means too much to her family."

Griffin puffed out his chest. "Valerie is sweet and kind. She may not like what's going on between Prince Jasper and Camilla, but that doesn't turn her into a killer. She wants what's best for her family. Don't put stupid ideas into her head."

"Bell's ideas are never stupid," Hodgepodge said from inside the backpack. "Better Valerie and Camilla know they're vulnerable than be blindsided when Lady Isolda hunts them down and strings them up in the courtyard after a fake trial."

A muscle twitched in Griffin's jaw. "That'll never happen. I'll watch Valerie. Nothing bad will happen while I'm around. Maybe I'm half the man I was, but I can fight. And I'll fight anyone from this family if they turn on Valerie."

"You're still all man." I gently touched his shoulder. "I can tell you're fond of Valerie and want to look out for her. Just don't let that fondness make you ignore problems."

"A problem being Valerie is deranged enough to pick up a knife and stab Prince Jasper in the back?" Griffin shook his head, a rare scowl on his face. "Don't you have dragons to look after?"

I stepped back. I'd never seen Griffin so surly. His alpha male side had reared up since he'd found a woman who'd taken his eye.

"Don't take his rudeness personally," Hodgepodge said. "Griffin is in love. Love brings out the worst in people."

Griffin scowled at the backpack but didn't contradict Hodgepodge. "I have work to do." He stomped away.

So did we. But while I worked in the collection room, I'd be thinking about which suspect to speak to next.

After work, I grabbed dinner with Hodgepodge, then we snuck to the concealed area of the forest where Emberthorn, Stormwing, and Juniper were tucked away behind a powerful blockade of spells and wards.

I updated them about castle events, and although they had a passing interest in the blade found sticking out of Prince Jasper's back, their focus was on Juniper and getting her baby back.

"Can we trust your friends to return my infant safely?" Juniper sat beside Stormwing with her front feet tucked underneath her, looking like a giant scaled cat. Her yellow scales gleamed, and her eyes were bright. She looked like a different dragon from the injured, shackled creature I'd met a few weeks ago.

"Judo is a show-off," Hodgepodge said from his favorite position on my shoulder, "but I'd be happy to go into battle with her. That cat has skills. Although there's something about her magic that tastes funny."

"We despise funny-tasting magic," Stormwing said. "It suggests an unstable character."

"Juno's magic is unique. I've never met a familiar with such old-feeling magic," I said. "It's not dissimilar to dragon magic. It's got that otherworldly, ancient feel to it."

"Which suggests she's hiding something about her power," Stormwing said. "It could be because it was gained illegally or summoned from a dark source. Cats are tricky characters."

"So are dragons," Hodgepodge whispered in my ear. "And grumpy."

"I heard that, lizard," Stormwing said.

"Juno must have been through testing trials being the familiar to such a powerful witch," I said, "but that doesn't make her bad. Her experience will be helpful in times of crisis. I trust her and her companion witch, Zandra Crypt. Have you ever heard of the Crypt witches?"

"The demon-hunting witches from Willow Tree Falls?" Emberthorn raised his head, finally interested in the conversation. He'd been snoozing on and off ever since we'd arrived.

"Yes. If there's a troublesome demon that Angel Force can't control, they call on the Crypt witches to deal with them. They've been guardians of the original demon prison in Willow Tree Falls since time began. Zandra is connected to that family. And she's powerful. Although I'm not sure she realizes quite how strong she is. She lets Juno do the tricky spells."

"Our sidekicks always underestimate themselves." Hodgepodge sniffed my cheek. "I'm always reminding Bell she's got decent magic, but she never believes me."

I flexed my fingers and grinned. "It's easy to forget when you don't use that magic often."

"That'll change when we're back in charge," Emberthorn said. "We'll lift magic restrictions and make sure people believe in their powers again and aren't fearful to use them."

"It's something we're looking forward to," I said.

"We must get my baby back first," Juniper said.

"They called her Cinder," I said. "Do you like the name?"

Juniper slow-blinked and tilted her head. "I believe I do. A fiery name."

"Named because she kept burning everything she looked at to a crispy cinder," Hodgepodge said.

Stormwing grumbled at him. "Show respect for your betters."

Hodgepodge craned his neck and peered through the trees. "I don't see them. Let me know when they show up."

"I will help in this fight, but I need to know Cinder is safe," Juniper said. "My mind is consumed with thoughts of her. I'm no use to you until she's back with me."

"She will be soon. I'm still waiting to hear from Juno about how their visit to Wild Wing went. If it wasn't a success, we may have to go with them and try again."

"We need you here," Emberthorn said. "With the chaos at the castle, Lady Isolda and her family will stop at nothing to get what they desire."

I couldn't resist a smile. "It's good to know you weren't sleeping the entire time I was updating you."

"I can listen with my eyes closed." Emberthorn bowed his head, acknowledging his preference for sleep than action. "We may have to move quickly when we see an opportunity."

"You're thinking of revealing yourself before the wedding?" I asked.

"From the way you're talking, the royal wedding won't happen," Stormwing said. "Someone will get it right the next time they go after Prince Jasper and snuff him out."

"We need to figure out who that someone is. I've ruled out Valerie Oldsbrook," I said. "I wondered if she'd attacked Prince Jasper to protect Camilla, but she was adamant the wedding had to go ahead for the benefit of her family and their war."

"A war they're losing, by the sound of it," Hodgepodge said.

"I'm not aware of this conflict," Emberthorn said. "So many memories are muddied because of our time encased in stone. When we're back in power, we can offer assistance to bring their battle to an end."

"Their problem is stuffy dragons who've lost touch with reality," Hodgepodge said. "Valerie said they're set in their ways."

Emberthorn puffed out smoke. "I've been accused of that a time or two. Mainly by my brother."

"They need a kick in the rump," Stormwing said. "I'm happy to help with that, but we deal with our problems first before offering help to others. We need a stable place to rule from and no threats to our own home."

"The second I know what's going on in Wild Wing, I'll let you know," I said. "And I promise, you'll get your baby back soon, Juniper."

Running feet had me turning swiftly, and I crouched, preparing a spell between my hands. Griffin appeared, flustered and out of breath.

"What's wrong?" I asked. "Do we need to move? Has someone learned the dragons are here?"

He glowered at me as he took in several deep breaths. "It's Lady Isolda. Warwick overheard her arranging an interrogation."

"For what happened to Prince Jasper?" I shook my head. "She can't arrest Camilla. She has a firm alibi."

"It's not Camilla who's in trouble." Griffin's fierce glare shocked me. "Valerie has confessed to attacking Prince Jasper. Bell, this is all your fault."

# Chapter 8

"Bell isn't responsible for another person's actions." Hodgepodge was quick to jump to my defense, his neck ruff flaring. "If Valerie confessed, maybe she is guilty."

"She wouldn't have even thought about confessing if Bell hadn't put the stupid idea in her head." Griffin simmered with fury. "After you left the stone chamber, she went quiet. I kept asking what was wrong, but she wouldn't tell me. Then she said she had something to do and left. The next thing I hear, Lady Isolda has her in custody and plans to question her."

My gut clenched, and I felt hot. "I never thought she'd do that. We'll go to the castle and explain everything."

"You'll do no such thing," Hodgepodge said. "If you march in there and say Valerie is lying, Lady Isolda will think you stabbed Prince Jasper."

I pressed my lips together. "Valerie is innocent. I'm sorry, Griffin. I didn't mean for this to happen."

He huffed out a breath, his anger still clear. "It's too late for an apology. But I need help to undo this mess. You must convince Valerie not to ruin her life to save Camilla."

I looked at the dragons, and Emberthorn nodded. "I'll come back to the castle with you. Do you know where Valerie is being held?"

"I heard she was taken to Lady Isolda's private quarters." Griffin grimaced. "You can imagine nothing good will happen up there. We'll find Warwick. He'll know what's going on."

I said a quick goodbye to the dragons and dashed away with Griffin, Hodgepodge resting on my shoulder, his tail wrapped protectively around my neck.

"Don't feel guilty," he whispered to me. "You were looking for answers. You didn't know Valerie could be so easily influenced."

"When we spoke, I wasn't thinking. It's clear she loves her sister, and she doesn't value herself," I said. "If Valerie believes she can save Camilla by taking the blame, she'll do it."

"It makes my blood boil, some of the things she told me," Griffin said, glancing over his shoulder as he strode ahead. "People can be cruel just because she looks different."

"Then they're idiots," Hodgepodge said. "Valerie is charming. And I see she's caught your eye."

Griffin acted as if he hadn't heard Hodgepodge's comment. "She has a good heart. It doesn't matter what a person looks like. It's their character that makes them attractive."

Now wasn't the right time to tease Griffin about his infatuation with Valerie, but once she was free, and we would get her free, I'd give him a nudge to ensure he pursued his interest in her. They both deserved happiness. Griffin had spent too long hiding from everyone since he lost his arm.

We arrived at the castle and hurried into the servants' tunnel, heading toward the main atrium, where Prince Jasper was attacked.

"We need to find Warwick," Griffin said. "He can help us sneak Valerie out."

"If we sneak Valerie out before Lady Isolda is satisfied she's innocent, it'll make her look guilty." I hurried beside Griffin, Hodgepodge now safely tucked inside his backpack.

"I know she's innocent. She couldn't have done this." Griffin stepped into the atrium and froze.

"Are you talking about my silly sister?" Camilla descended the stairs in a floor-length black dress, a sad look on her face.

"Do you know what's going on?" I gently pushed past Griffin.

She nodded. "I couldn't believe it when I heard Valerie had confessed to stabbing Jasper. She saves spiders, so I know she'd never get stabby, no matter how nasty the person."

Griffin narrowed his eyes. "Then who stabbed Prince Jasper?"

Camilla blinked slowly. "Gosh? Aren't you stern."

"This is a serious situation." I checked we weren't being observed then drew closer to Camilla. "Did you have anything to do with it?"

"I wanted to." Camilla plucked at the folds of her dress. "I've dreamed about killing Jasper plenty of times. But someone else got there first. Well done, them. Although it wasn't Valerie. I tried to speak to Lady Isolda, but she refused to see me. Hateful creature. She can't keep my sister as her plaything."

"We came to help Valerie get free," I said.

"Oh! Did you stab my horrible fiancé?" Camilla looked askance. "Bell! I didn't think you had it in you."

"It wasn't her. Or me." Griffin drew in a deep breath. "And I know it wasn't Valerie because she was picking flowers in the castle grounds. Lady Isolda requested a specific shade for your wedding, and the colors brought in by the florist were wrong. Valerie thought she knew the shade Lady Isolda wanted, so she went to explore to find a match to show the florist."

"How do you know all that?" Camilla asked.

Griffin looked away. "I watched her pick the flowers."

"You absolute creep!" Camilla grinned as she swatted at Griffin. "You're lurking about after my sister. Wait until I tell Valerie! She'll glow like a beetroot when she knows you're smitten with her."

"Beetroots don't glow," Hodgepodge whispered from inside the backpack.

"Valerie doesn't know the village well, and I didn't want her to get in trouble," Griffin muttered.

"No, no. You don't get away with this. I see exactly what's going on." Camilla waggled a finger from side to side, a conspiratorial expression on her face. "You're hopelessly in love with my sister and will do anything for her. And so you should. Valerie's the best person I know. Ten times better than me, and I'm lovely."

Griffin adjusted the front of his tunic. "I'll admit, I am fond of Valerie. I've never met someone with such a pure heart. She's always looking out for other people and making sure they're happy. But I know she's suffered.

She hasn't said much, but I've heard unkind words directed at her when people think she's not listening. Don't worry, I made sure those loose lips got firmly sealed, so they won't say anything stupid again."

"It's nice you're looking out for Valerie," I said.

Griffin shrugged, still not looking happy with me. "I'm glad I was. I can tell Lady Isolda that Valerie was nowhere near Prince Jasper when he was stabbed. She was outside the castle. And there were two gate guards who saw her, too. They were saying rude comments when she was bending over. I told them what they could do with those comments."

Camilla dashed forward and hugged Griffin. "You're my sister's Prince Charming. How wonderful she's found you. It's nice that something good has come out of this horror. I may have to marry that disgusting snake, but at least I'll know Valerie will be happy with you. You'll protect her, love her, and make her the happiest woman alive."

"They haven't even been on their first date yet," Hodgepodge muttered.

"We must tell Lady Isolda about Valerie's alibi," I said. "With Griffin and the gate guards as eyewitnesses, Valerie will have to be set free."

"We need Warwick," Griffin said. "He'll know how to handle Lady Isolda without making her suspicious."

"You don't need that gruff guard snapping and snarling at you," Camilla said. "Warwick is grumpy and no fun. I'll take you up to Lady Isolda's torture chamber."

"She has a torture chamber?" I glanced at Griffin.

"Most likely. I spend as little time in her rooms as I can. I insisted on going up when the guards took Valerie, though. Lady Isolda was furious with me, but there was nothing she could do about it. She wouldn't allow me inside and said I'd be an unhelpful influence, and she needed to speak to my sister alone to get the facts. I wasn't happy. I may have screamed. I could scream again."

"What did Lady Isolda do when you screamed at her?" I was part fascinated and part horrified that she'd acted so rashly.

"She slammed the door in my face and locked it with such powerful magic I couldn't break through. See, I broke a nail trying."

"That must have been painful." I didn't want to go to the private family quarters, but Valerie's innocence was at stake, and I felt partly responsible. Of course, Valerie didn't have to throw herself on Lady Isolda's mercy to save Camilla, but if I hadn't spoken to her, she wouldn't be in this situation.

"Follow me. If anyone asks why there are servants upstairs, I'll back you up. Although most people avoid me," Camilla said. "Honestly, I get the impression most of the castle staff are terrified of me."

"I can't imagine why," Hodgepodge whispered. "Leave while we can. Make a run for it, and Camilla will never catch you. Don't go up those stairs."

I gently shushed him. We had to do this. Griffin would disown me if I didn't help. And since we all knew Valerie wasn't Prince Jasper's attacker, we couldn't let her take the blame.

Camilla took the lead, singing softly under her breath as she skipped up the stairs and along the corridor. "It's the door with the two guards outside. Lady Isolda has all these rooms to herself." She flicked a finger back and forth as we passed half a dozen doors. "Goodness knows what she needs all the space for. One is definitely used for torture. Another may be a prison. She has a room for her dresses and furs, another room for her diamonds, but what else is she storing? She doesn't read, and since she's inhuman, I doubt she sleeps, so there won't be a bedroom."

I shook my head. Camilla always leapt over the line of suitable speech with the royal family. Was she fearless, or had she lost her mind? Right now, I just needed her to hold it together until we found Valerie and ensured Lady Isolda knew the truth.

Camilla stopped outside the door guarded by the stern-faced soldiers. "We have crucial information about the suspect. Eyewitness accounts that prove her innocence. We must be permitted to enter."

"Lady Isolda said no one can go in." The soldier on the left shifted from foot to foot, his gaze lit with anxiety. He must have encountered Camilla before.

"It's a matter of life and death. My sister is in there, and she's innocent. You will not stop me from seeing her." She shoved him, but he didn't move.

Griffin's attention was on the other guard. "We don't want trouble. And you know I wouldn't be here unless it was important."

This guard was older. A similar age to Griffin, with a large scar running across one cheek almost to his mouth. "I'd let you in if I could, old friend, but you know what the family is like. They'll string us up by our ankles if we break the rules."

"You know each other?" Camilla asked.

"We served together," Griffin said.

"Griffin used to be my boss," the guard said with a sad smile. "I've never had a better leader. We all thought what happened to you was wrong. I'd have said something, but... well, you understand."

"That's in the past," Griffin said. "But we need to get into this room. Lady Isolda has the wrong person. I know where Valerie was when Prince Jasper was stabbed. It couldn't have been her."

The door was yanked open. Lady Isolda bristled in front of us. "Camilla! I told you to stay away. And why are there servants outside my private rooms? Guards, have you lost the use of your senses? There can be no other explanation for why a stable hand and a serving maid are lurking on my finest carpeting."

"I brought them here," Camilla said. "I gave them permission to join me, so they're allowed."

"Oh, I apologize. Did I gift you my castle and forget?" Lady Isolda stepped into the hallway, her icy gaze slicing into Camilla.

Camilla didn't flinch. "Almost. When I marry Jasper, I'll be in charge as his equal. We'll rule side by side with no interference from anyone else."

Lady Isolda inhaled sharply, her nostrils flaring. "Is there something I can do for you, or have you come here to harass my guards and make a nuisance of yourself?"

"I have an eyewitness who saw Valerie at the time of Jasper's stabbing." Camilla pointed at Griffin. "Valerie was outside. She couldn't have done it. We've come to rescue my sister."

"And what is she doing here?" Lady Isolda glared at me.

I gulped. I hadn't expected to encounter Lady Isolda, so I had no cover story.

"Bell is a character witness," Griffin said. "She's willing to provide testimony as to Valerie's good nature."

Lady Isolda exposed her perfect white teeth. "Her testimony won't stand against scrutiny. Why would a servant's word be more influential than mine? If I say Valerie is guilty, then she's guilty. And if anyone wants to challenge that, I look forward to seeing how long they survive."

Camilla stamped her foot. "We have more than one eyewitness! Gate guards saw Valerie, too. How many people are you prepared to silence to fake my sister's guilt? I won't let it happen. I'll tell everyone what you're doing. Rumors spread like fire in this place. You'll be a laughingstock before the end of the week. Your son stabbed, and you tried to pin the crime on a sweet, innocent woman. You only have to look at Valerie to know she's incapable of violence. It'll be just another reason people consider you a fraud and unfit to rule."

Lady Isolda thrust her hands behind her back, but I didn't miss the magic sparking on her fingertips. She longed to attack Camilla, but the audience was too big for her to get away with it.

"Retrieve the gate guards who allegedly saw Valerie," Lady Isolda said to one of the guards. "I want everyone here. After all, we need to thoroughly investigate this case. The rest of you may enter."

It was the last place I wanted to go, but I couldn't refuse Lady Isolda, so I shuffled in behind Griffin, Camilla taking the lead again. The room was opulent and richly furnished. The paintings on the wall depicted curious scenes of impish figures in caves, dancing around fireplaces. The curtains dripped down the windows in a rich crimson, matching the cushions and throws.

I half expected to find Valerie shackled to a chair, but she was seated on a luxurious couch. When she saw us, the terror fled from her eyes, and she jumped to her feet.

"I thought that was your voice outside!" She rushed to Camilla and hugged her.

"These people are here to rescue you." Lady Isolda smirked as she paced to the window and stood with her back to it. "Apparently, my former champion thinks you're worth speaking up for."

Griffin kept his chin raised. "Valerie is innocent. I'll stand up in court to testify if I must, but I saw her outside the castle picking flowers at the time of the attack. She couldn't have been in two places at once."

Valerie gasped and stared at Griffin.

"Your words are worthless. I lost respect for your judgment the day you almost got my family murdered," Lady Isolda said.

"Speak to your gate guards, too," Griffin said. "You must trust their word."

Lady Isolda glowered at him before she flicked a look my way. "And this servant thinks you have such a kind nature you couldn't possibly be a killer. I suppose you're best friends, are you?"

Valerie stared at me with wide eyes. "I... I like Bell. I didn't realize she'd help me, though."

"I've seen nothing but good in Valerie since she arrived at the castle." I focused on Valerie and ignored the death-dagger stare from Lady Isolda for speaking up when I should remain meek and silent. "Why would she attempt to kill Camilla's fiancé?"

Lady Isolda inspected her fingernails. "I can think of one or two reasons."

There was a knock on the door, and after Lady Isolda announced they could come in, the older soldier entered, followed by two gate guards.

"I need the truth from both of you. Have you ever seen this woman?" Lady Isolda pointed at Valerie.

They looked at Valerie and then at each other.

"Well? Is she familiar to you?" Lady Isolda asked.

"She's hard to miss, looking like that," one of the guards said. "She was outside not so long ago, picking flowers."

Lady Isolda hissed her disapproval. "Did you say anything to her?"

"No, we just watched," the other guard said. "Had a bit of a joke. Nothing bad, mind."

"Leave us." Lady Isolda dismissed the gate guards, and they were happy to scurry away without incurring her rage. She pivoted on her heel and faced Valerie, who cowered away. "Liar! I should banish you and your sister. You're a disgrace for not speaking the truth. What did you think you would get from pretending you'd stabbed my son?"

"I... I..."

"She was playing a game." Camilla grabbed Valerie's hand. "We used to do it all the time back home. She doesn't understand how things work here, or she would never have been so silly. It won't happen again, will it, Valerie?"

Valerie swallowed loudly. "It won't. I made a mistake."

"A game?" Lady Isolda's expression showed her disbelief.

Camilla and Valerie nodded. Everyone waited to see if Lady Isolda would explode with anger.

She drew in a breath and exhaled slowly. "Go away before I set an example of you all. You've wasted my time, when I should be sitting by my grievously wounded son's bedside. Go."

We dashed out, but I didn't breathe until the door had shut and we were twenty feet away.

"That was close," Griffin said. "Did she mistreat you, Valerie?"

She shook her head, her body quivering.

"I'll look after her." Camilla grabbed Valerie's elbow and propelled her along the corridor. She looked back at me and winked. "Thank you. We'll have tea tomorrow to celebrate our win over old hag face."

We may have won this battle, but Lady Isolda was gearing up for all-out war against Camilla.

# Chapter 9

"What's this? Smells like ripe apples." Hodgepodge was near a corked vial of amber liquid that swirled on its own.

"Something powerful, which you shouldn't be near." I lifted him off the cabinet and set him on the floor. "If you knock something over, it'll go bang, turn us into ogres, or evaporate us. No more prodding immensely powerful magical artifacts, or I won't bring you along anymore, and you hate staying home alone."

"We should take some of these things." Hodgepodge ambled over to a pile of dusty spell books. "After our encounter with Lady Isolda yesterday, she'll be after you."

I set down the book I'd been dusting, careful not to open the pages and unleash any trapped spells. "Maybe. Fortunately for us, there were too many eyewitnesses to let her get away with what she had planned for Valerie."

"She must have been in a rare good mood." Warwick walked around the side of the bookcase. "I could tell you stories about guards who've vanished because they displeased her. On one occasion, Lady Isolda went out with a dozen of my best men, and only six returned.

No one would say what happened, but the squad was terrified. Most of them had nightmares for weeks afterward. One even resigned and took a job on a pig farm."

"I've never seen her in a good mood. The only reason we got out in one piece was because Lady Isolda didn't want to make a mess of her chamber by killing anyone." Hodgepodge nosed at a spell book until I distracted him with a piece of dried jerky.

"She gave up too easily. Lady Isolda still wants to pin the crime on Camilla," I said. "She didn't want to charge Valerie. Now Valerie is off the hook, Lady Isolda will be after Camilla again."

"And she's plotting something vicious," Warwick said. "I don't think she slept last night. My guards reported her pacing her room, talking to herself. Sometimes, she'd cry out and throw something at the wall. A guard checked on her and got hit in the head with a bronze statue. It gave him a concussion."

"Lady Isolda is losing control," I said. "She's lost the dragons. A mysterious attacker injured her only son, and the woman who was supposed to save the family is messing everything up."

"She's never been in full control of anything," Warwick said. "She rules by intimidation and fear. And that makes her subjects unhappy. They're scared, and scared subjects snap."

"Have you got any leads on what actually happened to Prince Jasper?" I asked.

"Nothing. No one saw anything. Which is odd because the castle is always busy. But the gate guards saw no one acting strangely. None of the servants saw anyone running away. It's as if whoever did it was already inside the castle, and they vanished the second they attacked."

"Sounds like magic to me," Hodgepodge said. "Look for a strong magic user. Someone unafraid to bend the rules."

"Whoever it was, they'd have needed to be fast and stealthy. I was wondering about Astrid. Maybe Evander," Warwick said with a smirk. "What trouble have they been getting into lately?"

"Don't joke about that," I said. "They're probably on Lady Isolda's suspect list. But they've got their hands full with Emberthorn and Stormwing. They don't have time to stab anyone."

Warwick checked the paperwork on his desk. "I'm worried Camilla and Valerie aren't safe. Valerie was lucky she didn't get slung in the dungeon for lying to Lady Isolda. And if it weren't for Grand Dame Ravenswood being Camilla's alibi, it would be over for her."

I rested a hand on the book, and magic pulsed along the spine. "Which means we need to find out who stabbed Prince Jasper."

Warwick arched an eyebrow. "Don't you have a different focus?"

"I keep telling Bell to manage one quest at a time," Hodgepodge said. "But she keeps getting distracted by wanting to help everyone. That'll end up in trouble, and then who'll be around to buy me pie?"

"I'll get it delivered to you if I end up in the dungeon," I said. "Emberthorn and Stormwing are focused on getting Juniper's baby. While they're so distracted, there's little we can do to prepare them for their return to rule. That mission needs total focus. We can't afford anything to go wrong when we reveal them."

"You've not heard from your friends yet?" Warwick asked.

I shook my head. "Maybe they've met resistance in Wild Wing."

"How are they staying in touch?"

I pulled out the small mobile snow globe I'd been carrying around with me.

Warwick took it and inspected it. "It's not switched on."

"It was!" I glanced at Hodgepodge. It must have gotten turned off by accident when we were looking at it.

Warwick shook it vigorously three times, and the device sparked to life. It buzzed and bleeped as he handed it back to me.

I looked at the screen. "There are five messages!"

Warwick disappeared behind the bookcase, chuckling to himself.

I read through each message. They provided updates about visiting Wild Wing and negotiating with the dragons.

The last one said: *Call us. ASAP.*

It took me a few minutes of pressing buttons before I figured out how to make a connection. A second later, Juno's large cat nose appeared in the globe. She zoomed out, and she was on Zandra's shoulder.

"Greetings! Have the dragons been keeping you busy?" Juno asked.

"They have. Sorry I haven't returned your messages. Slight hitch with my magic tech skills. It sounds like things are going well."

"Hey!" Zandra said. "We're making progress, but there is a ton of formal stuff to get through. We're attending a dinner tonight."

"A banquet in our honor," Juno said.

Zandra smirked and shook her head. "Forced social interaction and being nice to strangers. I'll grit my teeth to get through it. At least they're not making us dress up. We've got one more meeting to get through with the dragons, but after the dinner and the meeting, we'll be good to go. Is everything fine on your end? We were getting worried when we didn't hear from you."

"We're on track," I said. "It's been eventful here. Prince Jasper got stabbed."

"There's always someone wanting to take the throne of power," Juno said. "Was it fatal?"

"No, but understandably, everyone in the castle is on high alert. People are concerned."

"Concerned he survived?" Zandra said. "Everyone we've spoken to describes Prince Jasper as a giant snake. They don't trust him. No one in that family is trusted. None of the dragons here like the Ithric family. There are rumors flying around about them. None of them good."

"Then the rumors are true," I said. "How's Cinder?"

"Strong and excitable," Juno said. "And so big! Much bigger than me."

"When you're ready to move, it'll be safe to bring her to the dragon sanctum," I said. "There's no way anyone will locate her behind all the magic. And it'll be easier to move one small dragon than three full-sized ones."

"We'll let you know when we've got the final details," Zandra said. "Providing I survive this dull dinner and fake smiling all night."

"They're serving sea bass in my honor," Juno said. "It'll be a delightful evening of sea fish, scales, and storytelling."

I looked up as someone called my name outside the collection room. "Have fun. Got to go." I gestured for Hodgepodge to hide and tucked the mobile snow globe away just as Camilla appeared in the doorway.

"There you are! It's time for that afternoon tea. I have so many secrets to share with you."

The private dining parlor Camilla had commandeered at the back of the castle was small, intimate, and lavishly furnished in red and gold. We had seats close to a window, so we had a view of the grounds. And it was just the two of us, since I'd had to leave Hodgepodge behind.

"Here we are!" Camilla clapped her hands as a servant provided a sumptuous afternoon tea with plates of finger sandwiches, cream and jam-filled scones, and delicate fondant cakes topped with fresh cream.

"All this is for us?" I stared at the mountain of food.

"Of course. I shall have two of everything, and so must you." She heaped her plate as she waved away the server.

I chose a warm sweet scone and a sandwich. Then took a fondant iced cake, too.

"I'm so disappointed Jasper is still alive," Camilla said. "I visited his room earlier today. I didn't want to, but

Lady Isolda dragged me there, saying I must get used to supporting his every whim."

"Providing he does the same for you."

Camilla almost snorted cake out of her nose as she laughed. "That ignoramus only thinks of himself. I'm doomed to be his miserable wife. There's no way he'll die now, so the gruesome wedding is still going ahead as planned."

"Should I say sorry?"

She lightly tapped the back of my hand with a finger. "You can be as sorry as you like. I know I am."

"Has Lady Isolda made any progress in finding out who actually stabbed Prince Jasper?"

"Not as far as I know. Although she tells me nothing. Providing she doesn't keep looking at my sweet sister, that's all I care about."

"And you, too," I said. "Although you can't be surprised she was interested in you."

Camilla licked cream off her fingers and grabbed the largest cake. "And why would that be?"

"You enjoy talking about all the different ways you could murder Prince Jasper."

Camilla giggled. "True. It's my favorite hobby. I am cross with Valerie, though. I should have known she'd do this. When we were children, she was always protecting me. She's the best older sister. I'm glad Griffin was about to save the day, though. What a hero. And I never noticed how handsome he is."

"He's one of the good guys," I said. "It's nice he's connected with Valerie."

"A connection! What a stuffy way of saying they love each other. I'm thrilled for Valerie. She was either mocked or ignored back home. I did my best to protect her, but I couldn't catch everyone who was cruel. It's just a shame she had to come to such a dreadful place to find her soulmate."

"I'm glad they make each other happy," I said. "But give them time to get to know each other properly before you marry them off. Griffin has had his heart bruised more than once. And from what I know of Valerie, she's not one to let her heart lead her head."

"Only when it comes to me. She adores me as much as I adore her. Foolish thing." Camilla attempted to fit a mini cake into her mouth without biting it in half, leaving smears of chocolate on either side of her mouth. "Why not push? I had no time with Jasper. We met three times, and the deal was done. I didn't have any opportunity to grow fond of him. Not that anyone would. Have another cake."

I looked at the plate Camilla offered me and shook my head. I should sneak a treat out for Hodgepodge, but Camilla would ask me why I was taking it. He'd be so angry he'd miss this feast. I'd pretend the sandwiches were dry and the cake was full of raisins. He wasn't a fan of raisins.

"I know you like to think you're untouchable, but it's important we keep looking for the person who stabbed Prince Jasper. Lady Isolda is still displeased with you," I said. "I don't want you getting hurt."

"I'll never be hurt. I'm the solution to her problems. What will she be left with if she's foolish enough to get rid of me? One son dead, another was so repugnant no one else will touch him, and a crumbling kingdom. No one will want to rule that. She should be grateful I stepped into the role. Well, I didn't really step. My family decided for me, but you understand."

"It's a tricky situation," I said. "But it's important Lady Isolda trusts you."

"She trusts no one. Why waste my time trying to win her favor? When she's bouncing my first baby on her knee, she may be slightly less acerbic, but that's all I'll expect."

"I hope it works out for you." I masked the sympathy I felt for Camilla. Maybe this was an act, and she recognized her fate but refused to give in to the misery. Her future looked bleaker by the day.

"It will. Especially when I figure out how to finish Jasper off for good." Camilla held up a hand. "Since someone stabbed him, I should rule out that method of murder. I'm still thinking getting him drunk and pushing him off something high could work. But you highlighted the risks to me. A riding accident? Maybe he could be injured during a jousting contest. Do you have jousting contests in the village?"

"Not that I know of." Panic swirled inside me. "Camilla, may I give you some advice?"

"I'm always happy to listen to a friend's advice. Go ahead. How should I kill Jasper?"

"If you're really so desperate not to marry him, why don't you leave?"

A sour expression crossed Camilla's face. "If I could, I would. I must do my duty. I don't like it, and I won't be happy, but this isn't about me. You must understand. Say you understand. Then, say you'll be my flower crone. Did we settle on flower crone? I like that title for you. Wise and not ugly."

The door to the private dining parlor burst open, and a guard ran in. "My lady, we must move you to a more secure location."

Camilla was already on her feet, cake in hand. "Why? Whatever's the matter?"

The guard's gaze darted around the room, his magic staff fired up. "There has been another attack on Prince Jasper."

# Chapter 10

"Is he dead?" Camilla hurried toward the guard, a hopeful expression on her face. I was close behind her.

"I don't think so, but I don't have all the details," the guard said. "Lady Isolda is concerned that whoever is doing this may come for you. She sent me to find out where you were."

A smirk contorted Camilla's pretty face. "Of course she did. She was most likely hoping to find me with the weapon still in hand. Bad luck for her. Not only do I have my dear friend as my alibi, but there was a guard outside the room the whole time. I'm always being watched, and I'll be most happy to tell Lady Isolda I'm innocent."

The guard looked momentarily confused. "Lady Isolda is only concerned about your safety. She was most insistent I find you immediately and ensure your protection."

"It's an excellent cover story." Camilla looked my way. "Bell, I suggest you leave while you can."

"I can stay if you want me to," I said. "If you're right about Lady Isolda—"

"I am. But she'll most likely believe a guard's word over yours, given your lowly status. With luck, I won't even have to mention your name. Go. I'll deal with my dreadful mother-in-law-to-be and her false accusations." Camilla turned back to the guard. "You're absolutely sure Prince Jasper isn't dead? Did you check his pulse and breathing?"

The guard's expression grew cautious. "He's alive for now. Please, come with me."

Camilla tutted. "How unfortunate."

I hurried away in the opposite direction as the guard escorted Camilla along the hallway and out of sight.

Camilla behaved as if she had nothing to worry about, but I was concerned for her safety and now mine. Lady Isolda was noticing me, and that never brought joy to anyone's life. Despite how vast the castle was, I felt trapped inside the walls. I'd spent so many years keeping my head down, pretending there were no problems, and what I had was enough. I acted as if life was good and we had everything we needed. But I'd been hiding behind fear for too long.

Change was in the air, and although that was terrifying, it had to happen, even if that meant coming to Lady Isolda's attention. The realm was crumbling, and people were losing hope. And even though I felt Lady Isolda's hot breath on the back of my neck, circling me in the hope I'd be a useful pawn to destroy Camilla, I wouldn't be deterred. We were close to the end of this struggle, and the dragons would win. We were meant to have Emberthorn and Stormwing in this realm, looking after people and ensuring we prospered. No matter what it took, we'd make that happen.

I dashed to the collection room and collected a grumpy Hodgepodge. He spent several minutes sniffing my tunic as I carried him around, partly to comfort myself, but also because I'd missed him.

"You've been eating cake," he said. "Lots of different cake."

"Afternoon tea usually has cake. The cake's not important." I opened the backpack so he could climb inside.

He looked in the backpack. "It's empty."

"Sorry, Hodgie. I couldn't risk stealing cake in front of Camilla in case she asked questions. How would I explain my adorable wyvern has a sweet tooth? She'd insist on meeting you and then telling everyone about you."

"You should have said it was for you. Or better still, taken me with you. I hate being left alone. I deserved afternoon tea, too."

"What you deserve is to stay alive and not come to the attention of any Ithric family members. Camilla included. Hop in. I've got something important to tell you."

"Unless it has to do with cake, I'm not interested." Hodgepodge turned his back on me and thrashed his tail.

"It has to do with Prince Jasper being attacked again."

He instantly hopped inside the backpack, and as I walked to Seraphina's room, I updated him on the newest attack and the abrupt end to my afternoon tea. I also checked the mobile snow globe, but there were no new messages from Juno or Zandra. The sooner they got here, the better. We needed no more distractions.

"I take it this attacker also failed in their mission to murder Prince Jasper?" Hodgepodge asked.

"I think so, but the guard gave little away."

"It must be an amateur if they keep messing up so badly. I wonder if he was stabbed again."

When I arrived at Seraphina's study, I was surprised to find the door unlocked. She always kept her door locked. There were too many secrets hidden behind it to risk anyone creeping in and poking around.

I pushed open the door and walked in. There was no sign of Seraphina, although there was the usual jumble of unwashed mugs and plates on the table, so she'd been here recently. I called her name several times, but she didn't appear. Sometimes, she got absorbed in a book among her messy collections and lost track of time, blocking out distractions when she discovered a fascinating topic to devour.

I hurried along the book stacks, hoping to discover her, but all I found was more mess. A chair and table were knocked over, and books were spilled everywhere.

"This isn't like her." I picked up the dropped books and checked they weren't damaged. Seraphina would never treat books this badly. They were one of her passions.

"If someone has broken in, there'd be no way to check if they took anything," Hodgepodge said. "It's chaos in here. Only Seraphina understands the book stack logic. If there is any logic to her filing. And have you noticed that she sometimes smells the books to find the right one?"

I shook my head as I picked up the chair and table and set them right, a bubble of unease inside me. "You don't think she's been taken, do you? Lady Isolda could have discovered Seraphina's been going to the forest with healing potions. She could have been dragged away for questioning."

Hodgepodge grunted. "We can ask Warwick. He'll know if Seraphina's been slung in the dungeon. If she has been taken away, he was probably the one ordered to do it."

"Better him than a guard who doesn't know what's going on." I took one last look around then hurried out and shut the door.

As badly as I wanted to keep searching, I had to pretend everything was normal, so I dashed back to the collection room and set to work on a tray of potion bottles that were covered in so much dust and grime, I couldn't see what the labels said. Although I felt the power of the potions through the glass, so I handled them with care until Warwick returned to double check the magic.

"What if Lady Isolda suspects Seraphina of freeing the dragons? She'll force her to talk," I said to Hodgepodge.

"She'll try. Seraphina is more obsessed with those dragons than you are."

"Be glad I'm so obsessed. Otherwise, they'd still be trapped in stone." I set aside the first glass bottle. "Once we're done here, I need to make sure Camilla's not in too much trouble. The guard said he was taking her to a place of safety, but she figured out that was a ruse, and Lady Isolda is after her again."

Hodgepodge mooched around, poking his nose into things he shouldn't. "I know you want to protect Camilla, but you need to steer clear of her."

"I'm trying. It's not that easy when she's so demanding. And... I'd hate to be in her position. It must be awful, knowing you have to marry someone you despise to ensure your family doesn't suffer."

"It's why she's always got her head stuck in dream land. It's the only way to cope." Hodgepodge hopped away from a vase when it growled at him.

"At least we know she's not trying to kill Prince Jasper, since she was with me."

"Which isn't a good thing. You're her alibi! And you know what that means," Hodgepodge said.

"Lady Isolda could be after me? Camilla said my name in front of the guard, so he'll work out who I am, even if Camilla doesn't reveal all."

"Camilla isn't afraid of the royal family, so she'll say what she likes to them. That quirky lady could be the death of you," Hodgepodge said. "I know you feel sorry for her, but don't let her instability drag you down. When she tells Lady Isolda you were together, you'll fall under scrutiny. There'll be no more trips to the forest to see Emberthorn and Stormwing. It'll be too risky."

That made me pause. I didn't want to sever my connection with the dragons. It felt wrong, especially since they'd picked me to be their emissary. But if being around them put them at risk, I was willing to do it.

The mobile snow globe buzzed in my pocket, and I almost dropped the potion bottle I held. I still wasn't used to using advanced magical technology.

I carefully set down the bottle and extracted the globe. "It's a message from Juno. They're arriving tomorrow! And they're bringing Cinder."

"Progress at last," Hodgepodge said. "Once Juniper has her baby back, Emberthorn and Stormwing will focus on getting back to ruling. Then Lady Isolda won't be able to touch you. Or, if she does, Stormwing will bite her head off."

I stared at the globe for a few more seconds. Things were falling into place. With the dragons back in the realm, everything would soon be right again. Exciting times were coming, and I couldn't wait to be a part of it.

"Are you using my things?"

The globe slipped from my fingers and hit the table as an icy chill raked up my spine and dug into the back of my neck. I turned around. Lady Isolda stood in the doorway, the guard who'd been outside the private dining parlor beside her.

"Well?" Lady Isolda stepped into the room. "I don't employ you to use confiscated magic items. You clean them. That's your job, isn't it?"

I desperately wanted to check where Hodgepodge was. He'd been standing on the desk while I'd been looking at the mobile snow globe. He'd have had no chance to hide. I curtsied. "I carefully check each item before I clean it to make sure it doesn't get activated by accident. I don't know what most of these things do, so I don't want to make a mistake."

Lady Isolda held out a hand. "Give it to me."

I hesitated then lifted a potion bottle.

"No. I want that. Hand me the object beside it. Now."

I swallowed my panic and handed over the mobile snow globe. Lady Isolda inspected it for several seconds, turning it over. "I don't recognize this. But my collection is so vast, it's hard to keep track of everything we own." Rather than returning the globe to me, she handed it to the guard.

"Would you like me to leave?" I asked. "I can clean later if you wish to be alone."

"No. Stay," Lady Isolda said. "I understand you were both with Camilla when Jasper was just attacked."

I glanced at the guard. Although his expression was blank, his hand clutched his magic staff, the knuckles white with tension. "That's right. Camilla invited me to have afternoon tea with her."

"Why you?" Lady Isolda asked.

"I'm unsure. But she needed a companion, so I couldn't say no."

Lady Isolda glared at me. "Perhaps she's looking for a mother figure. An older, sensible woman who could guide her. Are you married? Has she been asking for advice on how to keep my son happy?"

I shook my head.

"Children? Has she asked you about raising a family?"

"No children. Perhaps Camilla felt sorry for me when she saw me cleaning."

Lady Isolda walked around the room until she was behind me. "You must have little joy in your life, since you're forced to do this kind of work."

That icy cold dug in deeper, and I resisted a shudder. "May I ask about Prince Jasper?"

"You may not. My son is none of your concern."

I bit my tongue. If I stayed quiet, she might leave me alone.

Lady Isolda returned to stand beside the guard. "Just so I'm clear. Camilla was inside the parlor the whole time Jasper was being attacked. Is that correct?"

I needed a second to stall and keep my composure. My knees wobbled. "When was the prince attacked?"

"Less than an hour ago."

I nodded, and so did the guard.

Lady Isolda turned, grabbed the guard's arm, and a swirl of grey, foul smelling smoke surrounded him. He groaned, fell to his knees, and hit the floor.

She looked back at me and lifted her chin in a clear challenge. "If you want to live, give me a different answer."

# Chapter 11

I stepped forward to help the guard, but Lady Isolda blocked my path. "Pay no attention to him. He made a mistake. I'm sure you won't do the same. I'll ask again. Did you have afternoon tea with Camilla today?"

My gaze went to the door.

"No! Answer me. Were you there when the guard entered and told Camilla that Jasper had been injured?"

A flicker of movement caught my eye. Somehow, Hodgepodge had gotten on top of a bookcase behind Lady Isolda. He was coiled, ready to spring, his teeth bared.

I discreetly shook my head. "Do you want me to say we weren't together?"

"Was my demonstration not clear enough? Forget you spent any time with Camilla. She didn't invite you to afternoon tea. You weren't in my private dining parlor, eating my food. And you have no idea where she was when Jasper was hurt."

Hodgepodge nodded at me, and the worry in his eyes made me pause, but I couldn't get the words out. Lady Isolda wanted me to lie, so Camilla would look guilty. With the guard out of action, Camilla had no one to support her story of where she was. Lady Isolda could claim she saw Camilla injure Prince Jasper.

"If you value what little you have, you will do this for me," Lady Isolda said. "Unless you want to become a mindless servant like this guard. Although I doubt I'll see much change in him. My guards are obedient. They do everything I tell them. This one, unfortunately for him, was too slow on the uptake to be of value, but I'll find some use for him."

I gulped to dislodge the knot of terror clogging my throat. I should tell her what she wanted to hear, so I'd get out alive.

Lady Isolda pinned me with a demonic glare. "So, what will it be?"

An icy wind swirled through the room, lifting Lady Isolda's hair and the hem of her floor-length gown.

She spun toward the door. "Who's there? Did you see someone come in? We aren't to be disturbed. Answer me, or you'll be sorry."

"There's no one else here," I said.

"Someone is following me! I'm convinced of it." Lady Isolda waved her hands in front of her face, as if dispersing smoke. "You must be able to feel it. And the smell. That disgusting old pipe smoke. Everywhere I go, it follows me."

Now I paid attention, there was a strange smell. As Lady Isolda complained and looked around, her eyes wild, Lord Frederick materialized. He winked at me then trailed Lady Isolda as she walked among the collection, muttering to herself and demanding answers.

"I know you're here. I sense your presence. When I get my hands on you, you'll be sorry you bothered me." Her tone was screech-tinged.

"Can't she see you?" I whispered to Lord Frederick as he swirled around the room.

He grinned as he passed me, giving my nose a tweak and leaving it numb. "She'll only see me if I want her to. And I don't want that old harpy to understand what's happening to her. You said you wanted me to talk sense into her. That failed, so I figured I'd have fun. Give her a taste of her own medicine."

"It's working." I was so grateful this ghost was distracting Lady Isolda from sealing my fate.

"Since you released me, I've spent time going around the castle. My head was hanging with shame and disappointment," Lord Frederick said. "And what has she done to my son? His illness is unnatural, and he reeks of toxic magic. I spent a few hours with him, and he talks in riddles and is convinced he's gravely ill and doesn't have long to live. It's all this one's doing. So, it's time she paid."

"Keep up the good work," I whispered. "And if you can chase her out of here, I'll be grateful."

"Consider it done. I'll have her locked in a turret before she knows it. She'll put herself there because she thinks she's going mad. She's ruined this realm. I'm confined to the boundaries of the castle, so I can't explore far, but if what I'm seeing inside these walls is a representation of what's going on out there, her rule must end." He swirled away, cackling laughter, and causing Lady Isolda to shriek as they made contact.

Warwick pushed open the door. His eyes widened a fraction as he took in the scene. He bent beside his fallen guard and checked his pulse before grimacing.

"Warwick!" Lady Isolda's tone was shrill. "To me this instant. Someone is playing tricks on me again."

Warwick glanced at me then hurried away to join Lady Isolda. Although I could no longer see them, I heard their conversation.

"This is unacceptable. We must deal with this," Lady Isolda said in a fierce whisper. "I demand you find out who is torturing me. I'll have their head."

"We have another witch visiting tomorrow," Warwick said. "She specializes in restless spirits and aura cleansing. If anything unnatural has attached to you, she'll unpick it."

Lady Isolda made a noise of displeasure in the back of her throat. "Another disgusting illegal to endure, full of false words. I suppose her fee is exorbitant?"

"You insisted on the best. The best is never cheap."

"The rest have all failed. Don't let her leave until she's cured me. I want it gone. The thing whispers to me all night. I feel like I'm going mad."

"That's the plan," Lord Frederick said cheerfully. "A few more weeks of this, and she'll be done for."

I almost felt sorry for Lady Isolda, but I hadn't seen her do a single kind thing since I worked at the castle. The ghost was right. It was no bad thing she was getting a taste of her own medicine.

Lady Isolda strode back into view. "Deal with that." She pointed at the guard. "And keep an eye on this one." She nodded at me then strode away.

Warwick closed the door and leaned against it for a moment with his eyes closed. "I'm not sure I can do this for much longer. Every day, she gets worse."

I glanced at Lord Frederick, who'd remained with us, and he nodded.

Warwick returned to his fallen companion and helped him into a seat. "Why do this? Billy was a good guard. She's messed with his head. I don't know how I'll unpick this magic."

"Billy told the truth. That was his only mistake," I said.

"What mistake? He was watching Camilla. Does Lady Isolda have a problem with that?"

I nodded. "She wanted us to lie and say we weren't with Camilla when Prince Jasper was attacked."

"That makes sense." Warwick sighed. "I can usually handle her moods, but she's been behaving so erratically."

"You can thank me for that." Hodgepodge jumped off the bookcase and landed heavily on my shoulder. He curled his tail around my neck.

"What did you do this time?" Warwick narrowed his eyes at me.

"Do you remember when Hodgepodge knocked over the urn of ashes and released Lord Frederick's ghost?" I asked Warwick.

"Of course. Wait. The ghost has been messing with Lady Isolda?" Warwick looked around. "Is he here? Why can't I see him?"

"He's here," I said.

"I'm not sure I trust this one." Lord Frederick jabbed a finger at Warwick. "He spends a lot of time with Isolda. Are they friends?"

"No, but Warwick has no choice but to protect her," I murmured. "Lord Frederick was true to his word. He explored the castle, hated what he saw, so he's doing something about it."

Lord Frederick swirled around Warwick, causing him to flinch.

"It couldn't happen to a nastier woman," Lord Frederick said. "She's fighting to keep her place on the throne while telling people she's ready to step aside. She'll never let go of the throne. Until she's dead, she'll fight."

"Have you overheard Lady Isolda talking about wanting to get rid of Prince Jasper?" I asked Lord Frederick. "If we can find evidence it was her, it'll be another nail in her coffin. The people are already having doubts about her. It won't take much more before they riot."

"No proof, unfortunately. She's a wiry one. Hasn't changed much since I was alive. But you must be careful around her," Lord Frederick said. "She'll destroy anyone who stands in her way. If she thinks you're a threat, you'll be gone too. Now, I have someone to scare. If you'll excuse me." He bowed to me and vanished.

"It must be Lady Isolda attacking Prince Jasper," I said. "Once he's dead, Camilla will have no value. Even better, if Lady Isolda frames Camilla for killing Prince Jasper, she can start a war with Camilla's family. Their backs are already against the wall because they're fighting on another border. Imagine the Ithric realm attacking, too. They'd be annihilated."

"It can't be Lady Isolda behind these attacks," Warwick said. "When they took place, she was in meetings. I guarded the door."

"Then Lady Isolda hired someone!" I said. "She paid an assassin to stab Prince Jasper, and when that failed, she got someone else to try. How was he hurt this time?"

"Someone tried to smother him in his bed."

I frowned. "Why not use magic?"

"Lady Isolda has restricted its use around Prince Jasper. There are wards around his bedroom that blunts magic. Even my staff doesn't work. It's basically a club." Warwick swung his magic staff through the air.

"Someone got into Prince Jasper's room without using magic, smothered him, and escaped without the guards capturing them?" I shook my head. "How?"

"Lady Isolda gave strict instructions that only two people were allowed to enter Prince Jasper's room: herself and Camilla."

"She is setting Camilla up!" I said. "Lady Isolda made sure she was in a meeting so she couldn't be implicated and is demanding I lie about being with Camilla to ensure she looks guilty."

Warwick didn't look convinced. "It's possible she hired someone, but there are ways into Prince Jasper's room if you know about the secret passageways. There are many in the castle that haven't been mapped."

"Like the servants' tunnels?"

"Yes. There are passageways that join some of the upper-level rooms to each other. Not many people know about them, though. Only family members." Warwick slumped against a bookcase. He looked tired. "If I hadn't witnessed Lady Isolda in that meeting, I'd be convinced it was her, too. And she'd want to do it herself. She enjoys death too much to deprive herself of such a treat. And she trusts no one else enough to believe they'd be capable of killing a prince."

I grimaced at that prospect.

Warwick's gaze hardened, and he pulled himself upright. "Bell, you need to leave."

"Leave this room?"

"The castle. It's too dangerous to stay," Warwick said. "Lady Isolda has noticed you, and nothing good happens to people who come to her attention."

"You're not doing too badly."

"I'm surviving. But trust me, I'm not thriving. The only reason I'm hanging on is because I know change is coming. If you hadn't released the dragons, I'd have given up by now."

"You were planning on resigning?"

"I planned on grabbing what I could and sneaking off in the middle of the night. Lady Isolda will never let me leave. I know too many of her secrets."

"Neither of us is giving up," I said. "I don't need to leave. Neither do you. What we need is to get the dragons back ruling and bring an end to this family's reign of terror."

Warwick's frown grew severe. "This fight will get messy."

"Bell is surprisingly stubborn," Hodgepodge said. "And although I'd much rather flee than fight, where Bell goes, I go. If she fights, I fight."

"And we're staying to fight," I said.

Warwick huffed out a breath. "Then we're all staying put. But on your head be it."

# Chapter 12

Seraphina paced the forest floor, her hands clasped together. She'd covered the same path for twenty minutes, alternating between gripping her hands tight and scratching the already red, flaky skin.

"They'll be here soon," I said.

"They're late. What if something's gone wrong?" Seraphina stopped walking and peered through the trees.

"They'd let us know if there was a problem getting away from Wild Wing," I said.

We received word that Juno, Zandra, and Cinder were on their way, so we made preparations to meet them in the hidden glade, allowing Cinder to be reunited with Juniper.

"Don't be so sure. Lady Isolda has spies everywhere. Someone loyal to the royal family could have snuck into Wild Wing. Your friends may be captured. Cinder could be in trouble."

"Juno has a dragon-sized ego, but she's not foolish," Hodgepodge said. "She'd fight her way out of any situation. Zandra is powerful, too. Trust them to bring us the dragon."

"I have no choice. We're so close to success, but it makes me sick to my stomach to think anything could go wrong at the last minute." Seraphina returned to her pacing.

I stepped in front of her and rested my hands on her shoulders. "You're exhausted and anxious. And the way you're still scratching suggests you've been clumsy with the healing potions again."

Seraphina hid her hands behind her back. "I am tired, but I can't sleep. Every time I close my eyes, hundreds of thoughts race through my head. And I still feel guilty about betraying Emberthorn and Stormwing."

"They've forgiven you."

"I'm not sure Stormwing has," Hodgepodge said. "He gets extra gassy when you're around. And that gas is always aimed in your direction."

I wrinkled my nose. The healing potion Seraphina gave Stormwing didn't agree with his digestion, and whenever I visited, I had to massage his stomach to release the trapped wind. It was a necessary but deeply unpleasant experience for everyone standing downwind.

"I'll spend the rest of my life in their service," Seraphina said. "I'll prove I've changed. I've matured. I acted like such an idiot, thinking the Ithric family would look after me. All they wanted was my knowledge. Then they trapped me in the castle. Not that I had anywhere else to go. It was a prison of my own making."

"Things are changing," I said. "Leave the past where it belongs. When Juniper gets Cinder back, it'll unite everyone. Stormwing may even smile. And I'm sure a young dragon will inspire Emberthorn to be a little more enthusiastic."

"He always was lazy," Seraphina said with a shy smile. "Don't tell him I said that."

"He is borderline useless," Hodgepodge said. "I figured he was sleeping so much because he needed to heal, but that's all he does. The last time we were all together, Stormwing bit his tail to get him to rouse."

"Sleeping is his favorite hobby," Seraphina said. "Always has been."

"And it'll be yours soon too," I said. "Once Cinder is here and safe, the other dragons will focus, and you can complete their healing. A few more steps, and we'll get them back where they belong. Then the realm can recover, and life will return to normal."

"It would be good to be able to close my eyes and relax," Seraphina said.

"I think all of us have been on edge ever since this began."

"When it's done, we're staying in bed for a week," Hodgepodge said. "We'll have our meals brought to us, get someone else to stoke the fire, and do nothing but sleep, eat, and read books."

"That sounds heavenly," I said.

A swirl of hot wind blasted the dried leaves off the forest floor and they swirled around us. There was a flash of white light, and Juno, Zandra, and Finn, with his hand resting on a stunning, shimmering white dragon, appeared.

Juno strode over and nodded at us. "Greetings! I bring you one beautiful, boisterous baby. Although don't call her a baby. She hates it. And just to warn you, Cinder is having control issues. It must be hormonal."

"Wow! She's beautiful." Cinder was about the size of a newborn baby elephant. As lovely as she was to look at, she'd be even harder to hide than Juniper's vibrant yellow scales.

Finn walked over with a curious youngster beside him. His pristine clothing looked singed, and he'd lost several wing feathers, but there was a big, delighted smile on his face. "Cinder, meet our new friends, Bell Blackthorn and her companion, Hodgepodge. And this is Seraphina Poldark. They're helping the dragons."

Cinder blew out a plume of white smoke and hopped from foot to foot, sparkling wings flapping behind her. "Greetings!"

"I taught her that," Juno said proudly. "In fact, I taught Cinder everything. She learned to eat when she lived with me, and we were about to begin flying lessons before she went to Wild Wing. I'm delighted with her progress. She's the perfect dragon."

Cinder bounded closer, tripped over her own tail, then grabbed Hodgepodge off my shoulder, and danced away with him as he yelped protests.

"Get off me, ya wee beastie! I'm not a toy. Don't make me put you in your place. I get mean, fast!" Hodgepodge hissed and growled.

"Cinder! That's no way to treat your new friends." Juno raced after them, Zandra not far behind.

"You'll need to make allowances for Cinder." Finn inspected his charred wing feathers and sighed. "She was impossible to control when she lived in Crimson Cove, and the Wild Wing dragons have overindulged her. She's also going through those difficult years as a young dragon, testing the limits. Watch out for the errant fireballs. She almost hit me in the face with one."

"I sense her power." Seraphina's gaze was on the youngster as she played with Hodgepodge, while Juno and Zandra pursued them and scolded her bad behavior. "Healing power, if I'm not mistaken, like her mother."

"The Wild Wing dragons think so," Finn said. "They've tested her abilities, and her strongest magic is healing. It's chaotic, but they consider her more powerful than most dragons."

"My potions and spells help Emberthorn and Stormwing, but to have another strong healing dragon join us will rapidly increase their strength." Seraphina's rapt attention hadn't left Cinder.

"That's if the little monkey doesn't burn this forest down before she meets them," I said.

"She's excited," Finn said. "And she was so happy to see Juno again. She didn't put her down for an hour!"

"How does she feel about meeting Juniper?" I asked. "Will they know each other?"

"Cinder will remember her mother. They communicated when she was in her egg, but they've never met in person. Well, dragon. This is the first time they'll meet snout-to-snout. It's only natural for her to be so excited," Seraphina said, a smile on her face.

I winced as Hodgepodge was tossed into the air.

He landed on Cinder's nose and shot smoke into her face. "Behave, or I'll pin you by the neck and make you sorry we ever met."

"She doesn't mean it." Juno was still in hot pursuit, the nimble dragon artfully avoiding her. "Be nice to her. Cinder's just an infant."

"She's a terror! Control your dragon," Hodgepodge roared.

"Let's take her to meet her mother," I said. "Juniper is anxious they're reunited. That may calm Cinder."

"I'd forgotten how much of a handful she was," Finn said. "But she sure is lovely."

"Still dragon-struck, I see." Seraphina was already walking after Cinder and the others.

"It's impossible to shake," Finn said. "We'll always be connected."

"Cinder will be grateful to have such a powerful angel on her side," I said.

Finn slung an arm around my shoulders and squeezed. "I'm glad you think so. And just so you know, I'm on your side, too."

"No touching! Unhand her, angel-demon." Hodgepodge bounced off Cinder's head and landed in front of me and Finn. He bit Finn's foot.

Finn jumped back and yelped. Cinder flew toward us, growling, flames flickering from her mouth.

I scooped up Hodgepodge and held him against my chest. "No! Everyone behave. No more playing, biting, or fire breathing. Everyone is excited, but we don't forget our manners."

Juno stared up at me and blinked. Cinder tilted her head from side to side as if considering how much of a threat I was.

"I am the dragons' emissary. Obey me."

"And I'm the emissary's companion," Hodgepodge said from the safety of my arms. "So, obey me, too. And that goes for you, angel-demon. No touching Bell without permission. My permission, not Bell's. She doesn't think rationally when you're around."

Finn chuckled as he twisted his ankle around several times. "No harm done. Everyone is anxious for this to go well."

"Let's get mother and baby back together," Zandra said. "Then everyone will be less on edge."

Finn caught hold of Cinder around the neck, his arm securing her by his side as he whispered in her ear. The dragon was taller than him and chunky. She could take him down if she struggled, but she calmed after eyeing me for several seconds. Seraphina walked just behind Cinder, discreetly examining her. Juno and Zandra fell into step with me.

"You could do a lot worse than Finn," Juno said to me. "He's a clever angel, loves animals, and he has his own apartment in Crimson Cove. A good job, too. Although the hours can be unsocial."

I blushed. "It's a tricky time to think about anything other than the dragons. Our realm has fallen into dire straits without their guidance."

"This problem won't always be here," Juno said. "As I keep telling Zandra, you can only dodge a perfect relationship for so long."

"What relationship am I dodging?" Zandra asked.

"A certain adorable tech mage who works at animal control," Juno said. "It won't be long before Randal is wearing a T-shirt saying 'I heart Zandra' to get your attention."

"You're terrible at matchmaking." Zandra stubbed the toe of her boot in the dirt. "Randal is a friend. Maybe Bell and Finn just want to be friends, too."

"I can tell that angel-demon wants more than friendship," Hodgepodge grumbled. "And Bell blushes and stumbles over her words when they're together."

"These days, he's more angel than demon," Juno said. "He's a fine companion, and I trust him with my life. I've heard you met his demon."

"It's a terrible creature," Hodgepodge said. "Too dangerous to be around Bell."

Juno flicked an ear. "I've also heard Bell was able to control the demon in a most interesting way."

"Stop stirring, Juno." Zandra lifted Juno and settled her on her shoulder. "Sorry. Juno has terrible boundaries. Everything is her business."

"It is. All I'm saying is that if Bell can control Finn's demon so effectively, they have nothing to worry about, and there's no reason why they can't unite," Juno said.

"There are lots of reasons," Hodgepodge said. "Mind your business, fluff ball."

Cinder lunged away from Finn. Her head shot up, her tail extended, and she gave a trumpeting roar. In the distance, a similar sound came back, and the ground shook.

"They sense each other," Seraphina said. "Look out, everyone. These dragons will only have eyes for each other, so there's a risk we'll get trampled."

We sensibly used trees as shields, just as Juniper appeared. She was closely followed by Emberthorn and Stormwing, who stayed a respectful distance back as mother and baby saw each other.

Juniper's yellow scales glowed and sparkled as she flung her wings wide. Cinder chirped and hopped then lunged at her mother and was enfolded in her giant yellow wings. They purred and chirruped and flapped their wings, joyfully reunited.

Emberthorn and Stormwing softly stamped their feet and slowly flapped their wings in a show of approval and pleasure that mother and baby were back together.

Juniper lifted her head and looked around the forest, a flush of deep joy coloring her scales orange. "It is safe."

We emerged from behind the trees and joined them, although I took it slowly, just in case any overexcited dragons forgot themselves and swooped a wing at the wrong second.

Juniper untangled herself from Cinder and lowered her head to the ground in front of Juno, Zandra, and Finn. "You have my eternal thanks for reuniting us. My heart is whole again."

"It was our pleasure to help," Juno said while perched on Zandra's shoulder. "She is a delightful infant."

"She's a giant bundle of excess energy, but it was worth getting fire singed to get you two back together," Zandra said.

Cinder set her head level with Juno, and the cat stepped onto the dragon's snout. "We hope to always be a part of your lives."

"By the looks of it, Cinder wouldn't have it any other way," Juniper said. "I consider you my family, just as she does yours."

Juniper looked over her shoulder at Emberthorn and Stormwing and gestured for them to approach. They were respectfully slow, and once they were close to

Cinder, they lowered to the ground and greeted her formally.

Cinder bounced over, clearly not remembering her dragon etiquette. She danced around Emberthorn and Stormwing several times, growling and nipping their tails. She stopped by their snouts, tilted her head from side to side, chirruped, and then appeared to kiss them both.

The second she touched them, a glow traveled over their heads, over their backs, and to the ends of their tails. The shimmering magic continued to trickle this path for several minutes, rotating over and through them.

"Look at that," Seraphina said, awe in her voice. "Cinder is healing them. She may not even know what she's doing, but it's instinctual. She sensed Emberthorn and Stormwing needed help and her ability took over."

"Like mother, like daughter." Juniper stood with pride radiating off her. "It's a strong ability in our line. We always want to help those who are injured. And we're stronger together. I'm so proud of my daughter."

"With Emberthorn and Stormwing healed, and Cinder back where she belongs, there's not much else to do before we're ready to move." Excitement and fear ran through me in equal measure at the prospect of finally righting all that was wrong in the realm.

"You need to storm the castle, remove the royal family, and get the dragons back in the seat of power," Zandra said. "Sounds like it might take more than a few minutes."

I smiled ruefully. "Well, maybe it won't be simple. Thanks for your help. What can we do for you in return?"

"We have everything we need." Juno leaped back onto Zandra's shoulder and booped her cheek with her nose. "Life in Crimson Cove is always perfectly busy. We are content."

"Stick around for a while longer," Finn said. "Things could get messy. And I know how much you love messy."

"We've already agreed to stay," Zandra said. "It'll be interesting to see how your dragons deal with the royal family. And things are quiet back home, other than some noise over that weird fungus festival being planned, so we'll hang out here and lend a hand."

Juno sighed. "Whatever my wonderful witch wants, my wonderful witch gets. And we have a knack for catching troublemakers. What do you need us to do?"

# Chapter 13

I'd arranged to meet Evander, Astrid, Griffin, and Warwick in a storage shed in the castle's yard the next day. It was the easiest and most discreet location I could come up with at short notice. I had to update them about the dragons, and we needed to plan our next move.

A small platter of dried meat and fruit served as lunch for Hodgepodge, while I had a cheese sandwich and a slice of blueberry pie. We were halfway through eating when Evander and Astrid crept in, closely followed by Griffin.

"No pie for us?" Evander grabbed for my pie, but Hodgepodge bit his finger to stop him.

"You're here to work, not eat," Hodgepodge said as he chewed on a piece of dried apple.

"Doesn't look like you're doing much work." Evander inspected his finger. "So, what's happening?"

"We're just waiting for Warwick to arrive," I said. "Lady Isolda is being difficult, so he needs to be extra careful not to be seen acting suspiciously."

"We know about Camilla getting into more trouble." Astrid leaned against the wall, a fresh bruise on her face suggesting she'd also been getting in trouble of her own again.

"I think Lady Isolda is behind the attempts on Prince Jasper's life, and she wants to pin them on Camilla. She despises her," I said. "Camilla is fearless. Always talks back to Lady Isolda and ignores orders."

"It sounds more like insane to me," Evander said. "Anyone who talks back to Lady Isolda gets in trouble."

"Camilla believes she's untouchable. But I'm worried about her," I said.

"You need to be worried about yourself." Warwick appeared and eased the door closed behind him. "You've gotten caught up in this mess."

"You need to take a step back." Griffin nodded in agreement with Warwick. "We can't afford to lose you so close to the finish line. The dragons depend on you."

"It's becoming harder to keep a low profile," I said. "I got entangled in Camilla's problems, and now Lady Isolda wants me to lie and say I wasn't with Camilla at the time of the second attack on Prince Jasper."

"She knows your name, and she's not forgetting it," Warwick said. "I still think you should leave while you can."

"We agreed I'm staying. And the dragons are almost ready," I said. "Wait until you hear how well the reunion went."

I updated them on Cinder's arrival and that we had two new magical recruits on board. A powerful cat and a strong Crypt witch on our side was a boost. The odds kept getting better that we could pull this off.

"It's good we have more backup," Warwick said, "but that doesn't improve your situation."

"I know. Which means we move now," I said. "Seraphina is running final checks on Emberthorn and Stormwing, but I'm sure they'll be ready any day. In the meantime, we contain the chaos in the castle."

"What have you got in mind?" Astrid asked. "Do you want us to storm the place and take out Lady Isolda? I'd be game. I'd love to wipe that sharp smirk off her face while stealing her jewels."

"Not yet. But we need to watch Prince Jasper to stop anymore attempts on his life," I said.

"The world will be a better place without him in it," Evander said. "The guy is no better than his brother."

"If Lady Isolda is trying to frame Camilla, we need to thwart all attacks," I said.

"We also need to watch Lady Isolda," Warwick said. "She's said nothing to me, but she could make a move on you. Bell, if you're a roadblock to her getting rid of Camilla, she won't hesitate. To her, you're no one important, and she'll think no one will miss you if you vanish."

"Just another nameless, faceless servant." Griffin cursed under his breath and shook his head.

I nodded. "It's a risk, but I'm staying. We also need to protect Camilla. Before you say you don't trust her, she's been thrown into this mess with no choice. She's made foolish moves, but she doesn't deserve to be ruined by this family. Camilla thought she was doing the right thing by joining the household, but everything is tumbling down around her. It's unfair."

"Camilla isn't your responsibility," Warwick said.

"We're still helping her," I said. "Camilla is as innocent as we are. She didn't ask for this. So, we're getting her out. Valerie, too."

Griffin nodded hard. "Valerie is too innocent to stay in this corrupt place."

Warwick grumbled then shrugged. "Bell's the boss. But I'm putting it out there that we don't need this complication."

I smiled. It was hard to believe I'd gone from invisible cleaner to leading a group of outcasts and supporting the dragons to return to power.

"Warwick, I need you to watch Lady Isolda," I said. "You have easier access to her than anyone else."

"I'll do it," he said. "But she grows more paranoid every day. Her lack of trust is making her hide things. And she's being driven to distraction by Lord Frederick."

"Lord Frederick? Isn't he dead?" Astrid asked.

"When we were in the collection room, Hodgepodge released his ghost by accident," I said. "He's been harassing Lady Isolda ever since he got out. It turns out she had a hand in Lord Frederick's death, so he's not happy with her."

Evander laughed. "That's just made my day."

"I'll do what I can to watch her, but she's making unpredictable moves," Warwick said.

"And I'll ask Juno and Zandra to sneak into the castle to keep an eye on Prince Jasper. They have no fears about using whatever magic is needed," I said.

"You're sure you trust them?" Astrid asked. "I don't like working with strangers."

"They're trustworthy," Hodgepodge said. "Annoyingly smug, but they know what they're doing."

"If the lizard says they're good, then who are we to argue?" Evander wiggled his fingers at Hodgepodge, who tried to bite them again.

I looked at Evander and Astrid. "I need you to ask around and see if there's any information on who wants Prince Jasper dead. I'm convinced Lady Isolda is behind the attacks, but we need to be sure. Once we know it's her, we focus our efforts on ensuring she doesn't get to him again."

"And you're staying out of the way," Warwick said to me. "Make sure you stay out of sight and hope Lady Isolda is distracted enough not to seek you out."

"Actually, I'll be watching Camilla with Griffin's help," I said. "We need to get her away from the castle. The longer she's here, the more vulnerable she is."

"And the more likely she is to say something else to enrage Lady Isolda," Hodgepodge said.

"I'm on board. But how can I help?" Griffin asked.

"You're an excellent horse rider," I said.

"Sure. Even one-handed, I'm one of the best in the castle. How does that help Camilla?"

"The collection room is closed tomorrow morning, so I'll have free time. I'll convince Camilla to go horse riding. If she thinks it's her idea, it'll be the perfect way to get her out of the castle."

"I don't figure Camilla as an outdoorsy type," Astrid said. "She wears those ridiculous silk gowns and shoes that get dirty as soon as she steps outside."

"I'll convince her how glamorous she'll look on a horse," I said.

"What about you, Bell?" Griffin asked. "I don't think I've ever seen you ride a horse."

"I don't ride, but I can figure it out. I just need a friendly horse. Are any of your horses friendly?"

Warwick chuckled. "Good luck with that."

"We have our orders." Astrid pushed away from the wall. "Let's get to work."

We snuck out one by one, being careful not to draw attention to ourselves.

Warwick paused by the castle entrance and pretended to adjust his magic staff. "Don't put yourself in harm's way. If Camilla proves to be a liability, let her take the fall. She's made too many mistakes around Lady Isolda. She's on her blacklist. I don't want your name there, too. I have influence over Lady Isolda, but not enough to save you if she decides you're meant for the dungeon. Once you're down there, I won't be able to get you out."

"You did before. You can do it again," I whispered.

"You're too trusting, Bell."

"I'm always telling her that," Hodgepodge said.

"We stick to our tasks and do our best," I said. "Let me know the second you hear anything worrying from Lady Isolda."

Warwick grunted and strode away.

Once Hodgepodge was safely hidden inside the backpack, I returned to work. We needed to put on a front for a little longer. But change flew toward us like a feisty dragon, and soon, there'd be nothing Lady Isolda could do to stop it.

I'd finished work later than planned, thanks to Hodgepodge letting loose a case of mummified beetles who'd come to life and attacked him. It took two hours to catch them and put them back. I was exhausted, hungry, and my clothes smelled of beetle dung. Who knew mummified critters could be so aggressive?

As we walked through the dimly lit streets back to our lodgings, an unsettling tension hung in the air. The village, usually alive with the hum of activity, felt deserted. My footsteps seemed louder than they should, bouncing off the stone walls and dwellings we passed.

"Have I said I'm sorry about the beetles?" Hodgepodge was curled around my neck.

I sighed. "Five times."

"Would a sixth time make you smile?"

I tickled his head. "I'll be fine once I'm clean and in my cozy chair with a mug of hot cocoa and a book. Today's been a trial."

"I didn't know the beetles would bite."

"I know you didn't."

"Or want to eat your flesh."

"Sure. Stop poking about in that room, though. If Lady Isolda had walked in and caught us trapping dangerous bugs, we'd have been in a world of trouble for touching her things."

"Tomorrow, I'll sit in the corner and not move. I'll barely breathe."

I'd believe it when I saw it, but Hodgepodge got bored while I worked, so I couldn't stay angry at him for being curious.

"What a lousy night," Hodgepodge grumbled. "Where is everyone?"

"No idea. There's nothing special happening this evening." I scanned the quiet road. The dim glow of the streetlights flickered sporadically, as if they'd go out at any second. There wasn't a soul in sight.

I quickened my pace, eager to be inside. The air grew heavier, and I couldn't shake the feeling that someone, or something, was watching us. I glanced over my shoulder, but the darkness swallowed any trace of movement.

We turned down a narrow alley, and the shadows played tricks on my senses, making it feel as if the walls were closing in around us.

Hodgepodge grumbled in my ear. "Hurry! I'm cold. Let's get home."

"Are you feeling it, too?"

"I feel my stomach grumbling."

"No! Something's wrong. There are no people around, and that... odd sensation. And I'm sure someone is on our tail. I keep hearing a scuffling, dragging sound behind us."

Hodgepodge stood and looked over my shoulder. He growled, making my spine tighten. My steps quickened as an indistinct snarl drifted through the air. I exchanged a troubled glance with Hodgepodge. He hissed in response to another snarl.

I picked up the pace, the urgency building with each echoing footstep.

A guttural growl echoed behind us, and something thumped against the wall. My heart pounded, and I grabbed Hodgepodge and broke into a sprint.

Heavy footsteps matched my pace. My breath came in ragged gasps as I darted through the labyrinth of alleys.

Something large crashed behind us, the vibrations shaking the cobblestone underfoot. I risked a look back and saw nothing but the darkness that devoured the narrow passage.

"Keep going!" Hodgepodge urged.

We turned another corner, and a low growl reverberated from the shadows. My muscles burned, and I pushed harder. The ominous growling turned into an enraged roar.

Without warning, something whizzed through the air, and a dull thud echoed as it struck Hodgepodge. He hissed in pain, his claws digging in to my shoulder so I didn't lose my hold on him.

I skidded to a stop, turning to face our unseen attacker, angry Hodgepodge had been hurt. My hands trembled as I conjured a protective shield, the hum of magic filling the air. Another projectile hurtled toward us, but my shield held strong, deflecting the lump of rock.

"Hodgie, are you okay?"

"I'm fine. Keep moving! This thing wants us dead."

We raced through the twisting alleyways, the growls and roars echoing behind us. A sudden impact against my back sent me sprawling. Pain radiated from my shoulder, and I gritted my teeth, pushing myself back to my feet. Another projectile hit me on the head, and I briefly saw stars.

"They're getting closer!" Hodgepodge still clung to me, his neck ruff extended. "I'll change and go after them."

"Not here. It's too risky. Someone will see you and report it to the family." I summoned a burst of magic, creating multiple shadows dancing around us. The growls stopped, our pursuer confused by the illusion, and we used the opportunity to change direction and put some distance between us.

We sprinted away, the echoing growls fading. Breathing heavily, I finally slowed and cast one last look over my shoulder. There was nothing but an empty alley and the lingering sense of danger.

"Hodgie, what the heck was that?" I ran my hands over him, glad to find no wounds. My shoulder throbbed, but the damage wasn't serious.

"Nothing we want to run into again. That must be the creature Warwick's been after." He sniffed my head. "You're bleeding!"

"It's not bad." I rolled my shoulder and winced. I'd have impressively painful bruises come the morning. "We're safe for now, but let's not hang around to give that thing another chance."

# Chapter 14

The morning presented me with a throbbing back, an aching head, and a desire to stay in bed all day. But I had bigger things to worry about than my bumps and scrapes.

After checking Hodgepodge, happy to see he had no ill effects from last night's attack, we grabbed a quick breakfast, and I dressed. Then we left our lodgings to search for Camilla.

She wasn't in the games room, eating breakfast in the dining room, or in the manicured grounds. I found her thirty minutes later, hiding in the back of the large family library.

"I didn't know you like to read," I said.

Camilla jumped then relaxed when she saw it was me. "I don't. Well, I enjoy a good romance, but who doesn't? Oh! What happened to you?"

"Nothing."

"Your head. You're bruised."

"An accident. I'm clumsy."

Her pretty blue eyes narrowed. "It wasn't our evil queen, was it? I've seen her beat servants."

I smoothed my hair over the injury. "No, Lady Isolda wasn't involved. Why are you hiding here?"

"I figured it would be the last place the monster-in-law would look for me."

"You're in trouble again?"

"Not for anything new." Camilla flung down her book. "That thorny old witch has it in for me. Apparently, I've been ordered to her rooms, but I refuse to go. I'm not a servant. She doesn't get to order me around."

"You need a break." I admired the leather bound books, careful to keep my backpack by my side, since Hodgepodge lurked inside.

"I wish! Everywhere I go, there's a guard watching. I had to run as fast as I could to get away from the last lot."

"You succeeded. They were looking for you near the dining hall. It took me a long time to find you, so no one knows where you are."

"You were looking for me?" Camilla beamed at me.

"I have the morning off." I glanced out of the large window. "It's such a nice day. You don't want to be stuck inside this whole time."

"I'd like to visit the dress shop again. But if Lady Isolda finds out, I'll be dragged back here and made to explain myself."

"What about a visit to the countryside? Fresh air, lots of places to hide."

Camilla tossed her blonde hair over one shoulder. "You know I don't like walking."

"What if you didn't have to walk?"

"Do you have a magic carpet I can ride upon?" Camilla giggled. "Wouldn't that be fun?"

"There are other ways to get around."

"I'd have to ask permission to take a carriage. And I'm not riding in a dreadful autobus thingy. The magic they use to propel them is peculiar. And they smell strange. As do the commoners on board. I could get a disease by breathing their fetid air. That really would make Lady Isolda's year. Killed by one of her subject's pox-ridden breath."

I continued inspecting the books. "What we need is a form of transport that gets us away from here quickly and allows us plenty of fresh air without lots of other people being around."

Camilla went quiet, her gaze blank. "Oh! I have the perfect idea. I haven't ridden since I got here. My horses have yet to be delivered. Do you think there are suitable horses in the stables?"

"Why don't we take a look?"

Her forehead wrinkled. "Lady Isolda can't see me. Give me your grubby cloak to wear, and no one will give me a second look. They'll think I'm a shabby servant on her break."

I unclasped my perfectly clean and decent cloak and handed it to her. "Keep the hood up, then no one will see your face."

Camilla swirled the cloak around her. Her nose wrinkled. "It smells of smoke."

"I have an open fire in my lodgings."

"This is more pungent than a log fire. I recognize the smell from somewhere. More sulfur than wood smoke. What is it?"

"Horse dung! I use it on my fire. It's free to use, so long as you shovel it yourself. The smell will soon disappear once you're riding a horse in the open air." Camilla could smell dragon smoke, and I didn't want her to get any ideas that I was friendly with dragons.

"How clever I am to have thought of this." Camilla flipped up the cloak hood. "I can escape for hours."

"We should take someone with us." I hurried us out of the library and along the corridor toward the stable yard.

"Not a tiresome guard. They'll report back to Lady Isolda and stop us having fun."

"No, not a guard. I have a friend who works in the stables. He's an excellent horseman and very loyal."

Camilla's eyes twinkled with amusement. "Is he your boyfriend?"

"No! Griffin is a friend. A good one."

"Oh! I know him. He's in love with Valerie."

I chuckled. "I believe he likes her."

"Of course he does. She's perfectly sweet. I'm happy to ride with him. He can be trusted, can't he?"

"Yes. Griffin used to work for the Ithric family, but there was an incident, and he lost his position in the royal guard. He was demoted to do general work in the yard, but he spends a lot of time with the horses."

Camilla glanced at me. "What kind of incident?"

"There was a raid on the royal carriages. He lost his arm protecting the family."

She turned and gaped at me. "How dreadful. They weren't able to save his arm?"

"They refused him any healing magic. It was his punishment for failing them. The family lost a number of valuable items."

"To prevent a man from receiving treatment is terrible," Camilla said.

"Griffin healed well. And he's excellent in the saddle. He also knows the best riding routes around here. And he won't breathe a word about what we're doing, so we'll be safe with him."

"Very well. He may come with us." Camilla sighed as we approached the exit. "You'll have to force me to come back, though. Lady Isolda will get what she wants eventually."

"What do you think she wants?"

A rare flicker of dismay darkened Camilla's features. "Me dead."

"Keep up, Bell. Your steed is barely moving." Camilla was way ahead of me, clearly an expert in the saddle, as she'd ably demonstrated as we'd ridden for five hours, following a route away from the castle and around the perimeter of a vast forest to the east of the village.

"Ignore her," I whispered to the horse. "Slow is perfect." It felt like bruises covered my body, and not the ones gifted to me by last night's incident.

People made horse riding look simple, but it was anything but. If you didn't get the rhythm right, which I often didn't, the hard saddle whacked me in places that shouldn't be whacked. I wasn't sure how I'd walk when I finally slid off the horse.

Fortunately, the horse was a good girl. Griffin provided me with a laid-back, calm mare, who was content to deal with an inexperienced rider. The horse did most of the work, happy to amble behind Camilla and Griffin as they showcased their talents.

Griffin rode ahead of me but behind Camilla, keeping an eye on us both. He dropped back to my side and smiled. "Having fun yet?"

"I'm in agony. How do riders manage this every day?"

"You get used to it. Muscles strengthen, and your form improves. How's the head?" He'd been worried when I'd told him about last night's attack.

"I barely notice it." The bruise on my back was much worse.

Hodgepodge growled from inside the backpack. "How is this fun?"

"It's not, but we've been able to distract Camilla," I said. "It's good to hear her laugh. And she only talked about killing Prince Jasper for the first half-hour."

Griffin smiled. "She hates that guy."

I gently encouraged my horse not to stop for another grass break.

"It's only a distraction, though, isn't it?" Griffin asked. "We can't stay away from the castle forever."

"It's tempting, but Lady Isolda will only send a search party and drag Camilla back." I leaned back slightly and peered around Griffin. There was a heap of gnawed bones on the ground. Beside them was a pile of rags.

Griffin turned to see what I was looking at.

"Who'd leave that here?" I asked. "Anyone living in the forest knows bones attract wild animals."

Griffin encouraged his horse closer and slid off. He bent and inspected the bones. "I don't know what kind of animal gnawed on these, but they had blunt teeth. Nothing with fangs would leave marks like this."

I somehow convinced my horse to get closer, although it was more by luck than skill, and stared at the rags. It was an old dirty tunic. Large, so possibly belonging to a man.

"You get odd types living in the forest." Griffin climbed back on his horse. "Maybe it was one of the many magic users the royal family has banished."

"What are you staring at?" Camilla had returned and stood up in her stirrups.

"Just rubbish someone discarded." What kind of creature had left these behind? And carnivores didn't have blunt teeth. Did this have something to do with the creature that chased us? Where was it now?

"I'll bury the bones to deter the animals." Griffin bundled the bones in the tunic, disappearing into the trees.

I kept watch for any trouble as I stayed beside his horse. Camilla joined me. Her cheeks were bright pink from the exercise, and she had a genuine smile on her face as she whipped her hair out of her eyes.

"This has been the best day I've had since arriving here."

"It was a good idea to come horse riding," I said. "We've blown away the cobwebs."

"It's been a wonderful day." Camilla gazed at the horizon. "Why don't we keep riding? We can head toward the setting sun, and I'll never have to see the dreadful castle or Prince Jasper again. Wouldn't that be wonderful?"

"If you want to make a run for it, I won't stop you." I meant it. If she stayed, Camilla's days were numbered.

She sighed. "It's tempting. But if you return to the castle and I'm missing, you'll get in trouble. People must have seen us together plenty of times, so they know how close we've become."

"That's unlikely," I said. "My superpower is invisibility. I keep my head down, my mouth shut, and stay out of trouble. I've worked at the castle for years, and most people don't even know my name."

"Not so much since I arrived." Camilla went quiet. "I know you think I'm a silly creature with no brain, but I was lonely until I met you in the stone chamber on that dreadful night when Prince Jasper got drunk and mean. You were kind to me. You listened. No one does that here. It's all barking orders and fear."

"It must be different from your old life."

Camilla's bottom lip jutted out. "I'd never tell my family this, but I made a terrible mistake by joining with Prince Jasper."

I turned in the saddle. "Talk to them. Tell them how bad it is. You have Valerie to support you, and she'll tell your family how terrible this place is."

"My sister is wonderful, but my parents pay her no attention. Because she looks different, they'll never be able to marry her off, so they see her as a nuisance. Even though she's helpful to them, they never listen to anything she says. I never noticed that until I came here, but it's a horrible place to find yourself." Camilla tipped back her head and closed her eyes. "The next time I see my parents, I'll tell them to change. They must be kinder to Valerie. I've done what they wanted, but that means they owe me a huge favor. And I mean massive. Being married to Prince Jasper will be gross."

"There are many people who see Valerie's true value," I said.

Camilla gave a snort, not dissimilar to her horse. "Everyone is obsessed with the way a person looks, or the kind of magic they do, but everything else is overlooked. It's about status and connections. When I'm in charge, there'll be none of that. Everyone will be welcome."

"It's a wonderful idea."

Camilla focused on me. "You think I'm afraid of Lady Isolda?"

"Unfortunately, I know you're not."

Griffin returned, wiped his hands clean, then hopped back in the saddle. "We should head back to the castle. If there's a dangerous creature out here, we need to be inside before it gets dark."

"I was telling Bell I intend to run away." Camilla laughed. "Both of you join me. We'll flee together, change our names, and no one from this realm will ever see us again."

"I can't come with you. I stand out in the crowd for the wrong reasons," Griffin said.

"If you're worried about your lack of arm, we'll do something about that." Even though Camilla talked about running, she turned her horse toward the castle. "I've heard of inventors who make incredible lifelike arms and legs. They use a special kind of magic, so they work almost as well as the real thing. Would you like one of those?"

"I don't need a new arm. I'm used to this." Although there was a flicker of hope in Griffin's eyes.

"When I'm your queen, it'll be one of my first jobs to give you an arm if you want one. I'm certain you looked after the royal family well, and they should have repaid you for your service, not punished you."

"That's nice of you to say." Griffin glanced at me, uncomfortable with the direction the conversation was going.

"I'm starving. At least that's one decent thing about the castle. You have an excellent cook." Camilla encouraged her horse forward. "I'll race you back. First one there gets two servings of dessert. Make that three!"

I groaned, my muscles protesting as I attempted to keep up with Camilla and Griffin, who easily outrode me.

"Slow down," Hodgepodge whispered from my backpack. "I'm getting motion sickness."

"I wish I could. But I can't lose sight of Camilla. Hold tight. This is almost over." I gritted my teeth and pushed on.

"What did you make of those bones?" Hodgepodge poked his head out of the bag and gulped in fresh air. "Were we supposed to be a meal? That thing hunting us through the alleyways last night wanted us for supper?"

I shuddered. "It can't be a regular beast. Something made with magic?"

"Where did it come from?"

"Let's hope we never have to find out."

After an hour of riding, I spotted the castle turrets. Something was wrong. Smoke rose from an upper floor window. The others had noticed it too, and slowed their horses.

"Is that coming from the private family floor?" I asked as I caught up with them.

"It is!" Camilla said. "It's close to Prince Jasper's room. Is someone trying to kill him again? I hope they got it right this time. Hurry! I want to see if my awful fiancé is dead."

I rode beside Griffin as we picked up the pace. "Do you think something's gone wrong? What if Juno and Zandra got caught watching Prince Jasper?"

"So they set fire to the place?" Griffin shook his head.

"What if they met their match with Lady Isolda and did something desperate?"

"We won't know until we get back." Griffin surged ahead on his horse.

Camilla was still in front of us as we approached the main gate. The cloak's hood had fallen back as she rode on, eager to find out what was going on at the castle. I called out a warning, but she either didn't hear or ignored me.

A guard appeared out of the gatehouse as Camilla's horse drew near. His eyes widened the second he recognized her, and he held out one hand, signaling her to stop. But she kept going. He slammed his magic staff on the ground, and a surge of power spread out around him, the tip of the staff crackling with energy.

"Halt! You're wanted by Lady Isolda," the guard bellowed.

Camilla slowed the horse and stared down at him. "She still wants to talk to me? She'll have to wait. I want a bath. I smell of horse. And then I shall require food. Lots of it. Riding works up an appetite."

Two more guards emerged from the gatehouse and strode over. Their expressions were aggressive, and their magic staffs crackled with energy. This looked bad for Camilla.

Griffin grabbed my arm and shook his head, a warning not to get involved.

"Come with us," the first guard said. He reached out a hand to Camilla to help her off the horse, but she swatted it away.

"I'm going nowhere. You know who I am, so let me pass."

"We know exactly who you are. That's why Lady Isolda wants you arrested." The guard grabbed Camilla's arm and yanked her off the horse.

She screamed as she hit the ground and they tussled. He jabbed her with his staff, and she yelled in agony and fell.

I jumped off my horse, my legs almost not taking my weight. I had to help Camilla. Griffin dismounted, too, but still held me back. He knew the risk of us being revealed.

"Camilla!" Valerie raced out of the castle and ran toward her sister, her face full of fear. Before she could reach Camilla, a guard shoved her back and she tumbled over.

Griffin abandoned me and dashed toward Valerie. A menacing guard cut him off. Griffin faced off against him, his fist clenched and shoulders set. Tension hung thick in the air, a palpable force that twisted my gut.

Valerie still lay on the ground, dazed from the unexpected shove, while Camilla struggled with the guards as they fought to keep her restrained.

Griffin unsheathed his sword, a glint of resolve in his eyes. "Let me pass so I may help the ladies."

The guard sneered at Griffin's defiance. "She's for Lady Isolda. You won't save her." Magic rippled around his fingertips.

Griffin's jaw clenched, his muscles taut with anticipation. "I'll ask politely one more time. Let me pass."

"Or what?"

He surged forward, sword cutting through the air with a lethal grace. The clash of metal echoed as sword met staff and magic shimmered.

The guard parried Griffin's expert blows as the air crackled with magical energy.

A chill slunk down my spine. This was too dangerous. Too exposing. A crowd had already gathered to watch the fight, and word would soon get back to Lady Isolda that Camilla had returned.

Griffin channeled his magic and sparks danced along his sword. The guard countered with a surge of energy that sent Griffin staggering, and he narrowly avoided a punishing strike from the guard's staff.

My heart raced as Griffin fought with everything he had, but in a decisive move, the guard unleashed a torrent of magic from his staff that sent Griffin sprawling, the impact of the spell reverberating through the gatehouse and making the crowd gasp and step back.

I clenched my fists and sent a silent plea for Griffin to rise. But he lay defeated and vulnerable. The guard towered over him, triumphant and merciless.

Valerie struggled to sit up, her eyes wide with terror. The guard turned his attention toward her, menace in every step as he approached. The air crackled with foreboding as he raised his staff, ready to strike her down.

I wanted to intervene, to defy the helplessness that gripped me. Griffin had fallen, and Valerie and Camilla's fate hung in the balance. I had to protect them.

"Don't move," Hodgepodge whispered. "If you get involved, Emberthorn and Stormwing will never return."

"Leave her alone." Camilla raised her hands, and an erratic blast of magic shot out and slammed into the guard's chest.

More guards surged forward, not hesitating in attacking. Camilla was whacked again and went down. This time, she didn't get up.

Lady Isolda marched out of the castle entrance in a swirl of righteous triumph. She grabbed Camilla by the hair and pulled her to her feet. "This is my son's attacker. There is nothing good about this deceitful creature. She manipulated a sick old woman and a feeble-minded servant to lie for her."

"Are you the feeble-minded servant?" Hodgepodge whispered.

I nodded discreetly. "And Grand Dame Ravenswood must be the old woman."

By now, an even larger crowd had gathered. Many onlookers appeared fearful, but some seemed excited as they watched the drama unfold.

"Camilla has betrayed us," Lady Isolda said. "She's manipulated others and repeatedly tried to murder my son. And despite her attempts at deception, I have evidence of her guilt."

My eyes met Griffin's. He was on his knees, a bleeding wound on his head. What evidence did Lady Isolda have against Camilla? If the smoke billowing out of the castle had anything to do with the latest attack on Prince Jasper, I knew it wasn't Camilla trying to kill him.

"Take this traitor to the dungeon." Lady Isolda shoved Camilla at the guards. "Her punishment will be swift and public. We will not have bad blood tainting our family."

I stepped forward, but Hodgepodge hissed a warning. "We can get her out of the dungeon, but we'll be no use to her if we end up behind bars, too."

It pained me to watch Camilla dragged away, still protesting, her hands bound. Griffin and Valerie were taken, too.

Lady Isolda swirled a finger in the air. "Get rid of this."

The guards sprang into action and swiftly dispersed the crowd. I attempted to sneak past, using the three horses as cover as I moved toward the stable yard.

"Not you."

I froze at Lady Isolda's cold tone. I remained hidden behind my patient mare.

Lady Isolda appeared in front of me and clicked her fingers. A guard hurried over and collected the horses, taking away my shields.

She sneered at me, her gaze icy and barren of any compassion. "You again."

I stayed quiet, my head lowered.

"I see now how close you are to Camilla. You lied to protect her, didn't you?"

I gulped. "I don't know what's going on. Does this have to do with the smoke?"

"You don't need the details. This isn't your home. You don't have a family to protect. Camilla is bad news. We're getting rid of her. Do you understand?"

I nodded slowly.

"And do you also understand what you need to do to ensure that happens? A poor marriage will not pollute this family. A mistake has been made, but I'm rectifying that. The sooner Camilla is gone, the better."

I bit my tongue.

"I'm glad we understand each other. If you show continued loyalty to me, you may come out of this alive." Lady Isolda turned and walked away. "Be in my private office in one hour. We have things to discuss."

# Chapter 15

"We have nothing to discuss with Lady Isolda." Hodgepodge had been wedged on my shoulder ever since the scary encounter by the gatehouse. His heartbeat was as fast as mine.

"She'll want to make sure I stick to the lies, so she can sentence Camilla for crimes she didn't commit." I paced my lodgings from the chair to the bed and back again. I'd been pacing ever since I'd escaped from Lady Isolda. Although it didn't feel like an escape, just a reprieve.

"She'll want to silence you for good," Hodgepodge said. "As her control lessens, she'll grow desperate to make sure any threat is removed. You're a threat!"

"I can lie! Make her believe I'm on her side."

Hodgepodge huffed in my ear. "Bell, you're a terrible liar."

"I'll do it if I have to. Whatever it takes to get Camilla and the others out of the dungeon."

"This is Camilla's fault. She should have kept quiet. Maybe she should have run when she had the chance," Hodgepodge said.

"She's loyal to her family," I said. "Even though it sounds like they don't treat her or Valerie well, she's obligated to support them. When you've been raised in an environment like that all your life, you can't think of any other way to live."

"Because of that, she's about to be put to death," Hodgepodge said. "You heard Lady Isolda. A swift public punishment. That means one thing."

My insides shook. "She'll execute Camilla in front of a watching crowd."

"And there's nothing we can do to stop it," Hodgepodge said. "We need to run. We can get out if we're quick. Start somewhere new."

"With what? I have little money. And we won't get far on fresh air."

"Take that big, dumb angel up on his offer to visit Crimson Cove. Once we're there, we'll stay. But we must move now. Lady Isolda will be expecting you soon."

"I can't leave. What about everybody else?" I asked. "I'm a dragon emissary. Emissaries don't run. They defend their dragons."

"They don't needlessly sacrifice themselves. We've done a great job getting this far. The dragons are almost healed. We've doubled their numbers, and they have other supporters. Emberthorn and Stormwing will understand why we left. They won't want you putting your life on the line for them."

"If we leave, Lady Isolda will hunt me. She sees me as a problem." I drew in a deep breath. "I should tell her everything. Tell her about the dragons, tell her about my role in getting them free. You never know. We may get lucky, and she'll die from the shock."

Hodgepodge snorted his disbelief. "That monster has a heart of stone. Nothing short of a dragon eating her will destroy her. Even then, I'm sure she'd give the dragon terrible indigestion. Bell, pack a bag and let's go!"

I shook my head, refusing to give in to my fear. "We must find out what's going on inside the castle. Was there another attempt made on Prince Jasper's life?"

"Who cares? And everyone else has probably been caught by now," Hodgepodge said. "Juno, Zandra, and Finn are probably already in shackles. And even if some of them got away, they won't expect you to wait for them."

"I don't believe that. Neither do you. You're saying it because you want me to find somewhere safe to hide." The trouble was, nowhere felt safe, not while Lady Isolda was still in power.

"I do! I want us to get out while we can." Hodgepodge dug his claws into my collarbone. "Don't visit Lady Isolda. It'll end in death. And not hers."

I paced some more, wringing my hands together. "I could make a deal with her. Offer her something."

"You have nothing Lady Isolda wants. Well, you have the dragons, but you'd never betray them."

"I could figure out a way to delay her. I could say I've got evidence about the person who's after Prince Jasper."

"She won't care. She only wants Camilla for that crime."

I chewed on my bottom lip. "What about the dragons? I could suggest I've seen them. Some place far from their haven. It could be enough to distract her from ruining Camilla's life."

"It could also enrage Lady Isolda. She'll know you've been keeping secrets, and she'll toss you into the dungeon along with the others."

"I need to buy everyone more time!"

"You need to get out of here."

I stopped by the window and looked out at my home. "No, we're staying. I need your help to find everyone. Lady Isolda won't have caught them all. Juno and Zandra must still be in the castle. They'll help you gather everyone else."

Hodgepodge growled his displeasure. "What are you going to do?"

"I must visit Lady Isolda. If I don't go to her, she'll send guards, and they'll drag me there. That'll only make things worse for me."

"It can't get much worse," Hodgepodge said.

I kissed his head several times and hugged him tight. "We need help. I know you don't like us being apart, but I'll make sure people see me going into Lady Isolda's office. That way, if she hurts me, rumors will spread about what happened if I don't come out."

Hodgepodge grumbled several times. "I hate this plan. It's a stupid plan."

"It's the only plan we've got." I set him down. "Now, go. Get the gang back together." I opened the door for Hodgepodge, and he scuttled away.

Camilla still had my lightweight cloak, and my winter cloak was too heavy for this time of year. I didn't want to look like I was sweating with fear when I met Lady Isolda, so I walked out of my lodgings in my tunic dress and headed to the castle.

It felt like a walk to meet my fate, and that fate was scowling at me and waiting to do battle with a spiked club in one hand and a dark spell primed in the other. I didn't know where Lady Isolda's private office was, but I discovered a heavy guard presence at the bottom of the carpeted stairs leading to the family rooms. I'd hoped to see Warwick among the guards, but there was no sign of him.

"Move along," a guard said when he noticed me lurking. "No one other than immediate family members access the upper levels."

"I have an appointment with Lady Isolda," I said. "She wants me to meet her in her private office."

The guard took my name, disappeared for a few minutes, and then returned. "Follow me."

I walked up the stairs, and two guards accompanied us. As hard as I tried not to appear nervous, my hands shook. The fear coursing through me would be interpreted as weakness, and Lady Isolda loved to play on people's weaknesses.

The guard knocked at a door and waited until he heard a voice on the other side. He entered and gestured for me to follow. The other two guards remained outside as the door was closed.

I was led to a room made entirely of stone. The walls were bare stone, the floor as well. There were stone shelves and a large stone desk. It was extraordinarily stark and unwelcoming. A perfect match for Lady Isolda's personality.

She sat behind the stone desk, and opposite her was a pretty, cowering girl who couldn't be more than twenty. Silky dark hair hung down her back, and she wore a form-fitting gown. Lady Isolda appeared distracted as she stood from her seat, and I could see why. Lord Frederick's ghost hovered by her left shoulder. His form was barely visible, but it became solid as he spotted me. He waved and winked then floated after Lady Isolda as she strode around the desk.

"If I have more questions, an aide will be in touch with your family." She gestured for the girl to stand.

The girl jumped to her feet, curtsied, then dashed away, the guard seeing her out before returning to the room and standing alert by my only escape route.

"What trouble have you gotten yourself into?" Lord Frederick asked me. "Put this one's nose out of joint by the looks of it."

I couldn't reply, but inclined my head at Lady Isolda.

"If you're on her wrong side, you're in trouble. Want me to scare her for you?"

"Tell me about your friendship with Camilla." Lady Isolda wasted no time as she settled back in her chair. "I've consulted with my guards, so I know you've been seen together."

I drew in a breath, attempting to calm my racing heart. "We've met a few times. It must be difficult being in a new place and knowing so few people."

"You wanted to befriend Camilla to gain access to my family's resources?"

"No! I'm happy with what I have."

"How can you be happy in your role?" Lady Isolda shook her head, her gaze darting around. "No, you want something from Camilla. You thought she'd gain you access to the inner circle. You picked badly. She has proven unworthy."

I remained silent and kept my gaze down.

Lady Isolda hissed and flew to her feet. "What do you want?"

My head shot up. "Nothing!"

"Not you. That whispering voice. Do you hear it?"

Lord Frederick cackled a laugh as he spun around Lady Isolda.

I shook my head. "I'm sorry, I hear nothing."

He swirled around Lady Isolda several more times, tugging on her hair and clothing. "Who knew that being dead could be so entertaining?"

Lady Isolda backed away, her eyes wide. "You must give evidence against Camilla to prove her guilt. I'm planning a public trial in the morning. She's a diseased thorn in my side, and I'm removing it once and for all."

"Any evidence I give won't be worth listening to," I said. "As you've made clear, I have no position of power. No one in the castle will believe anything I say. My name and word carry no weight."

Lady Isolda's eyes narrowed to flinty steel. "You're supporting me. No one will go against my word. If I say I believe you, everyone else will. And if they say otherwise, they know the consequences of such an unwise move."

I felt backed into a corner where the walls were spiked with poisoned barbs. "What do you want me to say?"

A flicker of satisfaction hardened Lady Isolda's face. "Camilla claims she was riding with you and the stable boy."

I nodded, although Griffin was no boy, and Lady Isolda knew that. It was her way of belittling his importance.

"I want you to say she lied. Camilla was here. She didn't leave the castle all day. You even saw her behaving erratically. Maybe you asked if you could help her, but she was unkind to you."

I pressed my lips together. It made me sick to my stomach that Lady Isolda was spinning me into her lies to ruin Camilla.

"After Camilla taunted you, you followed her. You were concerned about her well-being. I imagine you're an annoying, kindhearted type who always does the right thing." Lady Isolda smirked then yelped as the ghost pinched her arm.

"Is everything okay?" I asked.

"It will be once Camilla is gone. She's brought a curse with her. Godric is gone, Jasper has had three attempts made on his life, and I'm bothered by this... this thing! It's all because of Camilla."

"There have been three attempts on Prince Jasper's life?" I asked.

Lady Isolda glowered at me. "You saw the smoke. Camilla set fire to a rug in Jasper's room. I want you to say you broke the rules and followed her to the private family quarters. Of course, you'll be punished for such behavior, but I'll ensure it's not too painful. Anyway, you saw Camilla enter Jasper's room, and a moment later, you smelled smoke."

That lie would get Camilla killed. "What about the guards? There must be guards looking after Prince Jasper. They won't have seen me or Camilla near his bedroom."

"My guards say anything I tell them to," Lady Isolda said. "Confirm the story. Tell me what you saw."

I gripped my hands behind my back. I couldn't lie. "I was riding with Camilla. It's likely plenty of people saw us. If I claim I saw Camilla go to Prince Jasper's room just before the fire started, the lie won't be believed."

Lady Isolda stalked over to me, magic sparkling on her fingers. "If we support each other, a hundred people will confirm seeing you. And if they question you, they're easily silenced."

I opened my mouth to protest. Lady Isolda slammed a spell into my chest, and I hit the floor. Pain lanced through me, prickling across my skin and digging into my bones.

She stood over me. "Perhaps it would be simpler to kill you. I can find someone else to tell the exact same story. Someone with more credibility. You're worthless. You're nothing. Why did I waste my time on you?"

The door slammed open. Warwick loomed in the doorway, unable to hide his surprise.

"Warwick! Perfect timing. I have something for you to dispose of." Lady Isolda raised her hand over her head, darkness flickering in her eyes as she prepared a punishing spell.

Warwick's gaze flicked to me. "Not her. She's too valuable. She knows about your missing dragons."

# Chapter 16

I pressed a hand against my heart, fearing it would burst out of my chest in shock. Had Warwick turned traitor? Or had he always been on Lady Isolda's side?

"What could this servant know about my dragons?" Lady Isolda still had her hand lifted, swirling jagged sparks of grey magic around it, about to fire at me.

"Bell worked in the stone chamber for years," Warwick said with confidence.

I recognized the familiar tick of tension in his jaw muscles. He was nervous.

"I've had many cleaners work in that chamber," Lady Isolda said. "This one is no different from the others. Unskilled, fearful, weak. She has no sway over the dragons."

"Do you remember Clarice Blackthorn?" Warwick asked.

Lady Isolda's eyes narrowed a fraction. "She's hard to forget."

"Bell is her daughter."

What was Warwick doing? Why was he bringing up my mother in front of Lady Isolda? While she'd caused trouble for the royal family while alive, their paths never crossed. She'd been a cleaner, too, so far below her radar, despite the trouble she sometimes stirred.

"Why did I not know about this until now?" Lady Isolda lowered her hand, her fiery anger shifting to Warwick.

"Bell has followed in her mother's footsteps." Warwick stood straight, his gaze never once settling on me.

"A troublemaker who's obsessed with dragons?" Lady Isolda sucked in a breath. "I recall those symbols Clarice used to scrawl in the courtyard to summon the dragon energy. Foolish woman, thinking she held sway over them. They must have thought she was a joke."

"Not the troublemaker part." Warwick rested his staff on the floor. "But Bell demonstrated a natural way with the dragons. I've watched her clean. She talked to them and would sing to them."

I stared up at Warwick in alarm. I knew he was stealthy, but I had no clue I'd been under scrutiny for such a long time.

Lady Isolda's smile held no kindness. "Your mother thought she had a connection to the dragons that would lift her from a life of drudgery. It did her no good. She's dead, isn't she?"

Warwick nodded.

"You see. I'm always right. Rotting in the ground is no success."

I opened my mouth to protest, but a warning look from Warwick kept me silent. "Some people think they can bond with dragons. They believe in the old ways of the dragon riders."

"Then they're deluded. There's no magical link. Dragons occasionally pick favorites. Gift people long life and extra magic." Lady Isolda glared at me. "I see the similarity now you've pointed it out. Were you close to your mother?"

I nodded. "It was just the two of us for a long time."

"No father?"

"He left when I was young."

"I suppose he was unable to move past the betrayal." A cool slice of a smile slid across Lady Isolda's face.

I couldn't help but ask. "What betrayal?"

"Your mother and my husband." Lady Isolda adjusted her long skirts as if removing an invisible layer of dirt. "Before he went mad, Crosby could be charming. And, of course, he ruled the realm, so no one refused him anything he desired. He had a healthy appetite for all things."

"I don't believe you," I blurted out.

Lady Isolda loomed over me again, fiery hatred burning in her eyes. "Are you calling me a liar?"

"It couldn't have happened." My throat felt like it was closing. "My mother was always too busy to have an affair. She worked in the castle, and—"

"Spent most of her time causing unnecessary trouble. Yes, I'm remembering Clarice more clearly, the more we dredge up the past. She ran an illegal publication that printed lies about my family, suggesting we weren't fit to rule and didn't treat the dragons kindly." Lady Isolda bared her teeth. "As if they needed kindness. They're ancient beasts forged in fire. We must control them, not pander to them. Otherwise, they run amok. We did what we had to do to keep order. Yet your mother printed lies to turn people against us."

I had no clue what she was talking about. But my mother often disappeared for hours and was always vague about where she'd go when I asked her. And she'd always had a rebellious side, often keeping me up late as we'd talked about the family and how they ruled.

When I was younger, my parents had often argued, but I'd never understood why. Then my father had left. I'd forgotten how difficult things had been between them. Were the fights about her affair with Lord Crosby? I couldn't believe it. I wouldn't.

"I won't have the daughter of a deceiver in my castle," Lady Isolda said. "Warwick, get her out of my sight and put her on tomorrow's trial list. She can stand with her new best friend."

"Bell may know something valuable about the dragons," Warwick said. "She spent so much time with them."

Lady Isolda tapped her foot on the floor. "You mean once they'd been immortalized in stone?"

Warwick confirmed her question with a nod. "It was the way she talked to them, as if she considered them alive. It was unsettling."

"I always thought her mother was insane, so it must run in the family," Lady Isolda said. "This is a waste of time. Bell refuses to obey me. Like mother, like daughter, I suppose."

"Let me question her," Warwick said, helping me up.

"Why bother? Her twittering around the dragons means nothing. She has no value to them. Take her to the dungeon."

"Bell would visit them outside of her normal working hours," Warwick said.

"Because she had no life outside of work."

"She was there the night the roof was damaged."

Lady Isolda had been heading to her desk. She stopped and turned. "Tell me more. What did you witness that night? Who helped the dragons?"

I glared up at Warwick. What was he doing? Why was he revealing my secrets? The more information he leaked, the more trouble I'd get into.

"Answer me!" Lady Isolda strode over until she was so close I could smell her sour breath. "What did you see that night?"

Warwick tightened his grip on my arm.

"The damage! There was a hole in the roof. And there was glass and wood all over the floor," I said.

"What caused that destruction?" Lady Isolda's eyes gleamed with anger.

"Did someone steal the statues?" I asked. "They weren't there. They couldn't have been gotten out any other way."

"Why would someone want to steal two enormous stone dragon statues?" Lady Isolda drew in a breath and held it.

I cautiously lifted one shoulder. "You'll have to ask whoever took them. I was shocked when I discovered what had happened."

"So shocked you were unable to raise the alarm and let anyone know the statues had been taken?" Lady Isolda pursed her lips. "Were you involved in the theft? If you were obsessed with the dragons, perhaps you got it into your ill-educated mind that they belonged to you and you wanted them for yourself."

"Bell doesn't have the resources to steal anything, let alone the statues," Warwick said.

"That's right! I wouldn't know where to hide them. And I have no friends who would help me do something so risky. They'd know what would happen if they got caught."

"Share me your pitiful story of existence." Lady Isolda raised a hand. "Since the statues are gone, your work here is also finished."

"I still clean. I was assigned to your collection room," I said.

"Ah. Of course. I remember catching you snooping." Lady Isolda glanced at the desk. The mobile snow globe sat there. "You don't work there anymore, either. You don't work for me at all. And Warwick, I should fire you, too."

Warwick bowed his head. This wouldn't be the first time he'd heard those words from Lady Isolda.

"You're both idiots and incompetent," she said. "Why hide this information from me?"

Warwick lifted his head a fraction. "I've been investigating. I've already questioned Bell to see what useful information I could learn."

"And you didn't see fit to share that knowledge with me?" Lady Isolda raised a hand and blasted a spell into Warwick's chest.

He staggered back with a groan and sank to one knee as the magic swirled around him. "My apologies. You've been busy with other matters."

"You're a fool. I should make an example of you. I can't trust anyone. They lie to me, steal my dragons, or bother me with curses." Lady Isolda looked around the room, but Lord Frederick had stopped pestering her and was watching, a frown on his face.

"My lady, what would you have me do?" Warwick asked.

"Get up!"

He forced himself to stand, both hands gripped on his staff to help support him.

"I want this mess tidied." Lady Isolda waved a hand in the air. "How are the arrangements with Camilla's trial?"

"All set for tomorrow," he said through gritted teeth.

"Good. Ensure my subjects know attendance is mandatory. I want everyone in the village to see what happens to a traitor. It doesn't matter their rank, their situation, or their perceived privilege. If they disobey me by not showing up, they'll face dire consequences."

"I'll ensure everyone knows," Warwick said.

Lady Isolda's gaze flicked to me. "Question this one again. But no more mistakes this time. Get every ounce of useful information out of her and then make sure she never talks again. Do we have an understanding?"

"I'll make sure it happens."

Lady Isolda brushed her palms together. "Good. And after these loose ends have been tied, we'll have the wedding right after Camilla's trial." She strode back to her desk and looked through some paperwork.

I looked up in surprise. Who was Prince Jasper to marry?

"Which candidate did you find most suitable?" Warwick asked.

"None of them. What was the name of the last girl?" Lady Isolda asked.

"Lady Sophie Gilslade," Warwick said. "The Gilslade family owns a large estate in Tumbledown."

"They're wealthy?"

"Incredibly. And they have six daughters, so they're keen on finding suitable matches for them."

"Sophie seemed meek and young enough to not be trouble," Lady Isolda said. "Arrange for Seraphina to examine her. If she's deemed fit, she'll be Jasper's bride."

Warwick nodded again, his expression blank, even though I was certain he must be in pain, since Lady Isolda's magic still shrouded him and flickered across his skin in jagged waves.

"Ending Camilla's existence will be my gift to the happy couple. Once she's gone, the castle will feel settled. The curses she brought with her will be destroyed," Lady Isolda said. "She has delivered nothing but darkness and trouble. Maybe it was Camilla who stole the stone dragons. What do you say, Bell? Would you reveal all if you saw your troubled friend making off with my dragons?"

I longed to yell at Lady Isolda and tell her what a horror she was, but if I revealed my true feelings, I wouldn't get out of this room alive. So, I copied Warwick and remained quiet.

"Get her out of my sight," Lady Isolda said, a note of disgust in her voice. "And don't come back until you have something useful to tell me."

Warwick grabbed my arm, and we marched out. He closed the door and kept marching.

"What are you doing?" I snapped at him.

"Not here. I need to take you somewhere safe."

"Nowhere is safe now. You exposed me to Lady Isolda. What was she talking about, my mother and Lord Crosby? It can't be true. My mother never strayed. They had their problems but—"

"Not now, Bell," he growled out through clenched teeth. "We have bigger things to worry about."

He continued marching me along the corridors, down the stairs, and toward Seraphina's room. He knocked on the door, and a few seconds later, it was opened. I shoved past him, eager to talk to Seraphina and get away from Warwick.

But Seraphina wasn't there. It was Evander who'd opened the door and ushered us in. And he wasn't alone. Hodgepodge, Astrid, Evander, Finn, Juno, and Zandra were there.

"I did what you asked." Hodgepodge jumped onto me and settled on my shoulder. "By some miracle, everyone survived."

"Your faith in us is touching," Astrid said.

Evander looked uncharacteristically tense. "We heard about Griffin being taken."

"Camilla and Valerie, too." I looked around the group, and my resolve to see this through hardened. "Lady Isolda is close to the truth. Thanks to Warwick, she now knows I'm involved and I know something about the dragons. Why do that?"

"I had no choice but to reveal something of value about you," he said. "She would have killed you and thought nothing about it. But now she thinks you have information, she'll keep you alive."

Did I believe him?

Warwick sighed, sensing my caution. "I'm on your side. It was a stalling tactic. When I don't return and give her useful information, she'll order your execution, too."

"I thought you'd already ensured that would happen," I said.

"Trust me, I'd never betray you or the dragons," he said.

"Warwick can be a humorless jerk, but he's standing with us," Astrid said.

"I agree. With the humorless jerk part." Evander shrugged. "I back him, too."

"So do I," Hodgepodge whispered into my ear. "If we're doing this, we need all the help we can get."

I took a few seconds to calm myself. Warwick was right. He'd bought us time. I looked around the group again. This was it. We made a move now, or this quest would fail.

"Bell, what do you want us to do?" Finn asked.

The others waited for my reply.

It was time to finish this fight. "We ensure Emberthorn and Stormwing come home for good."

# Chapter 17

"I thought we'd have more time." Emberthorn stood alert in front of me, all traces of his usual relaxed demeanor gone.

After my brush with death by Lady Isolda's hand, I'd spent the rest of the day with Finn, Juno, Zandra, Evander, and Astrid, working through ways to deal with the royal family and introduce Emberthorn and Stormwing with the least amount of bloodshed.

A sleepless night had followed before we returned to the dragons' hidden sanctuary to update them. Warwick had remained at the castle to monitor Lady Isolda and warn us if trouble was coming.

"We need no more time," Stormwing said with a decisive snort. "We're ready. Thanks to Juniper and Cinder, our healing is complete."

"It's almost complete," Emberthorn cautioned. "Or did you mean to hit me with that fireball earlier?"

"I'm out of practice! It's not my fault. I've been encased in stone for years. I won't miss when I'm face-to-face with Lady Isolda. She's the perfect target."

Juniper softly soothed him with a few quiet words.

"Where's Seraphina?" I asked. "She wasn't at the castle, so I assumed she'd be with you."

"She's not here," Stormwing said. "And I'm glad of it. We don't need her interference anymore. Not now we have Juniper and Cinder."

"We've needed her interference every step of the way," Emberthorn said. "Seraphina is important to us."

"I'm worried about her," I said. "When I went to her rooms, it looked like they'd been turned over as if someone was looking for something. I wondered if Lady Isolda had ordered a search."

"You have nothing to concern yourself with," Emberthorn said. "When Seraphina is ready, she'll come back to us."

"Do you know where she's gone?" I asked. "We need her here to check you're ready to return to the castle. The Ithric family won't go quietly, so this could get messy. I need to ensure you're strong enough to fight."

"It will get messy when I snap a few family members up and gobble them down like the greasy little piglets they are," Stormwing said.

"Please, not in front of the baby," Juniper murmured.

Cinder seemed nonplussed to hear Stormwing talk about eating the royal family like they were pork wieners at a hog roast and was happy chasing Juno around the trees.

"My apologies," Stormwing muttered. "This has been a long time coming. I'm excited to remind the family how foolish they were to think they could get rid of us. We don't need Seraphina to give us the all-clear to do anything. We are ready. We can go now."

I held up a hand, and Stormwing stilled. "If we rush in without making a plan, this will end in disaster. I don't want anyone injured."

"Injuries will be unavoidable," Emberthorn said.

"Then no fatalities!"

Emberthorn inclined his head. "We will try our best."

"Bell's in charge," Evander said. "She gives the orders."

Stormwing snarled at him but didn't disagree. My emissary role meant something to the dragons.

I'd talked through the final plan as we'd made our way to the dragon sanctuary, but it didn't stop me from feeling concerned when so much was at stake.

"Griffin, Valerie, and Camilla will be in the dungeon," I said. "Before we do anything else, we get them out."

"Couldn't we sneak into the dungeon during Emberthorn and Stormwing's arrival?" Astrid asked. "Everyone will be staring at them when they descend in a blaze of fire and smoke. They won't notice us releasing prisoners."

"If things go sideways when Emberthorn and Stormwing arrive, I don't want Lady Isolda to panic," I said. "She's planning a public execution for Camilla this morning, and I'm worried she'll drag Valerie and Griffin into that as well. We need them clear of the dungeons and away from danger."

"I know a few ways in to the dungeon that won't be met with much resistance," Evander said. "I'll tag-team this with Astrid. She's snuck into the castle plenty of times and gotten away with it."

Astrid smiled as she held up her hands. "I'm saying nothing."

I nodded. Evander and Astrid were the right mix of stealthy, fearless, and smart to pull off this part of the plan. "Lady Isolda is planning the wedding immediately after the execution. She even sent some poor girl to be examined by Seraphina to ensure she's suitable to be Prince Jasper's new bride."

"She'll be out of luck since Seraphina's missing," Evander said.

"At this late stage, I doubt Lady Isolda cares what the tests reveal. She's desperate to put on a public show of solidarity and prove to the realm she has everything under control." I rested a hand on Hodgepodge's side, his presence calming me. "We can't let the wedding go ahead. It's insanity. The girl who's been chosen as Camilla's replacement is vulnerable."

"More fool her for putting herself forward to be the replacement bride," Astrid said.

"I doubt she had much choice," I said. "From what I heard, she comes from a large family, and they're keen to get the girls married and off their hands. And she's young. Barely twenty, if that. It's not fair for her to get mixed up in this messy situation."

Zandra arched an eyebrow. "Once the prisoners are broken out, the guards will raise the alarm, and that'll stop everything while they restore order."

"You're suggesting we won't be discreet during our dungeon heist?" Astrid asked.

Zandra shrugged. "I don't know you. Maybe you've got two left feet and fall over every time you try to be stealthy."

Astrid smirked. "I can look after myself."

"So can my wonderful witch." Juno jumped onto Zandra's shoulder and away from Cinder's excited snap-chase. "And she'll be happy to give you pointers if your nerve fails you. She has slain demons, defeated evil, ensured the world—"

"They get it, Juno. We're awesome." Zandra's cheeks colored as she stroked Juno to stop her bragging about their achievements.

"I say we fly over the castle, do a big reveal, and I drop onto Lady Isolda's head," Stormwing said. "Everyone will be so shocked that we can open every cell in the dungeon, and no one will stop us."

"Your desire to eat the royal family is strong," Emberthorn said. "But if you go in wings flapping and fire spouting, it'll cause terror. People will be killed in the panic. They aren't used to seeing dragons. We were trapped in stone for such a long time that we've become a myth. People are forgetting how important we are to the realm. And stone dragons returned to life will startle many."

"Sadly, we've gotten used to living under this tyranny," I said. "I agree with Emberthorn. The people have suffered enough. When you take back power, do it peacefully."

"I will get a chance to eat Lady Isolda, though?" Stormwing asked. "She's behind all of this. She sent most of her family mad. Killed anyone who spoke out against her and had the audacity to trap us as if we were pets in a zoo."

"And she shall pay for those crimes," I said. "But she can't pay if she's dead."

"Being eaten by me is a suitable enough punishment," Stormwing said.

Juniper gently nudged him with her head. "Less talk about destruction and more focus on how you will rebuild this realm. Once you and your brother are in charge, there'll be much for you to do. You'll have to unpick years of toxicity that have made many people give up hope."

"And you need to lift the curse," Hodgepodge said.

"What curse?" Juno asked.

"Since the dragons disappeared, there have been no babies born in the realm," Hodgepodge said.

"That's not a dragon curse," Emberthorn said. "Not our curse."

"It's a coincidence?" I asked. "Everything prospered under your rule, but once you were trapped, everyone became barren."

Emberthorn huffed a slow plume of smoke. "We are powerful, but we don't have god-like abilities. We balanced the environment so everything flourished. If we saw an imbalance, we remedied it."

"I'm not saying I don't believe you," Astrid said, "but you vanished, and no one has fallen pregnant since you left. Human or animal. And it's affected the whole realm. You can go to the farthest reaches, and it's the same story. No babies."

"That wasn't done by our wing," Stormwing said. "Besides, we were attacked without warning, weakened by magic, and wrapped in stone. It happened so quickly that we had no time to prepare such a complicated curse. And how would we sustain it while trapped and weak? The lack of new births isn't our doing."

"Whoever is doing it likes everyone to believe you're responsible," I said. "Some people have fallen out of fondness for you as the rumor flourished you stopped any babies being born."

"If I had to wager all my lunchtime brownies for the next month, I'd say your ruler, Lady Isolda, is behind this baby scam," Zandra said. "What better way to turn people against the dragons and accept her rule than by circulating a lie about a dragon curse?"

"I agree with the witch," Stormwing said. "Let's put it to a vote. I eat Lady Isolda, and the problem goes away. Maybe if she's dead, the curse will lift. A sorceress can only keep her magic active when alive. Kill the queen, kill the curse."

"No voting and no eating," I said. "We reveal you calmly and figure out how to break the curse when you're back in power. We start by rescuing Griffin, Valerie, and Camilla and make sure they're safe. Nobody is getting left behind."

"I usually favor shock and awe," Evander said, "but the villagers are unsettled. There's still talk of an unnatural creature terrorizing the streets."

"We almost met it," I said. "It chased us the other evening when I left the castle."

"Did you get a look at it?" Evander asked.

"We didn't see it, but we heard it," Hodgepodge said. "It's big, fast, and growly. And it wanted to eat us."

Evander nodded. "No one has seen it, but whatever it is, it makes terrifying moaning sounds."

"There have been more reports of peoples' yards being destroyed," Astrid said. "Not just messed up, but stamped into nothing. Although that could be drunk ogres losing control. There's a group of workers out near the bridge. They're rabble rousers once they finish work."

"Ogres get clumsy when they're drunk, but they're not mean," I said. "Or if they are, it's only with each other. They keep to themselves."

"The less chaos we cause when we start our coup, the better," Evander said. "It's like a stuffed tinderbox out there, waiting for someone to toss a match in. With the freaky night creature, Lady Isolda barking orders and terrorizing everyone, someone taking shots at Prince Jasper, and the general misery that's swept through this village, the less drama, the better."

"You're getting soft," Astrid said. "You're always up for a flash of heroic glory."

"Maybe I'm growing up. It's about time you did, too." Evander went to touch the bruise on her left cheek, but she shoved his hand away.

"We'll support your plan," Emberthorn said. "If you want your companions safe, we begin there."

I looked around the group and nodded. "I'll fly in with Hodgepodge. Hodgie, are you up for going super-size?"

"Anything for you," he said. "And I want you on my back. I don't trust those two. Not after I saw their last dismal performance."

"Don't make me trim those wings with my teeth," Stormwing said.

"You need not fear about our flying ability," Emberthorn said. "We've been practicing, and we're much stronger than the last time we took to the wing with riders on our backs. We won't let Bell down."

"I know you won't," I said. "But we'll need magic to hide us when we fly toward the castle. I was hoping Seraphina would have something to conceal us."

"Use your magic," Hodgepodge said. "You've grown stronger every day since Emberthorn and Stormwing awakened. You can easily cast an invisibility spell over all of us and barely break a sweat."

I flexed my fingers. I'd been feeling my magic grow, but it still felt alien to use it.

"You can do this, Bell," Emberthorn said. "Now we're stronger, you'll be stronger too. We're bonded. Our power is your power, and your magic is ours. We feed off each other and only grow more powerful. Trust in dragon strength. It is yours, as well."

"I'll do my best," I said. "Finn, Juno, and Zandra, I need you to focus on the wedding."

"I enjoy a good wedding," Juno said. "The chance to celebrate someone's special day."

"There's nothing special about this wretched day," Stormwing said. "Not when the mother-in-law is a monster."

"Focus on getting to Prince Jasper and his new bride, Sophie. Do whatever you need to get them out of there," I said.

"We're still going to rescue Prince Jasper?" Evander asked. "He's as bad as the rest of his family."

"We all agreed. And Lady Isolda is trying to kill him," I said.

"So let her kill him," Astrid said. "One less problem for us to deal with."

"She wants him dead and to pin the murder on Camilla. Camilla has her faults, but she's only marrying into this family to help hers. She's gotten in too deep and is in trouble," I said. "Prince Jasper also has no clue what's happening to him. He's a terrible person, but he doesn't deserve to be killed by his mother because she's hellbent on creating instability so she can cling to a throne she should have been kicked off years ago."

Zandra shrugged. "If you need us to get him and the bride out, we can do it."

"Do we need to worry about magic wards around the castle?" Juno asked.

"There are no specific wards in place. People are usually too full of fear to break the rules. But be careful. I don't know what Lady Isolda has planned." I blew out a breath. "Are we missing anything? We have to be prepared for whatever gets thrown at us."

Finn rested a hand on my shoulder and leaned toward me. "You've got this. You know what you're doing."

Hodgepodge smacked him squarely in the face with his tail. "That's close enough."

Finn backed away, rubbing his jaw, while Evander and Astrid chuckled at Hodgepodge's feisty protectiveness.

"When do we make the first move?" Emberthorn asked.

"As soon as possible," I said.

A pained groan came out of the forest, and I tensed.

Seraphina lurched into view. She was pulsing, hot sparks firing from her skin as she staggered from side to side.

I pushed past Finn to help her, but Stormwing swept me off my feet with his tail, and I landed on my back, the wind knocked out of me and Hodgepodge rolling in the dirt. "What's wrong with you? She's injured."

"Seraphina is fine," Stormwing growled. "Keep back while she goes through her change."

"What change?" I tried to get up, but Stormwing pinned me with his tail.

Hodgepodge snarled, glaring daggers at Stormwing. He was about to fly at him when Seraphina exploded.

# Chapter 18

I came to and found myself on my back again with Hodgepodge flopped against my chest. I lifted my head, letting out a relieved breath as I saw neither of us was injured, just stunned by the explosion.

My movement roused Hodgepodge, and he looked around, blinking slowly. "What in the name of all things dragon was that?"

I clutched him against my chest as I rolled over and sat back on my heels. The rest of the group looked equally dazed as the explosion must have rippled out and hit them, too.

There was no sign of Seraphina, but standing in her place was a sleek grey-scaled dragon with red sparkles around its neck and large gleaming dark green eyes. I stared at the dragon, and it stared back at me.

Hodgepodge hissed, launching out of my arms and super-sizing midair, crashing down in front of this unexpected arrival. He stamped in front of the dragon and swiped his tail at it.

The dragon didn't respond. It stood there, watching me. It looked like it was waiting for something.

Juno ran over, still the size of a slightly plump house cat, but the magic swirling around her was dazzling, and I had no doubt she was more than a match for this new dragon if it proved to be a threat.

Still, the dragon didn't respond. It kept looking at me and then turning to Emberthorn and Stormwing, who had shielded Juniper and Cinder during the explosion with his large wings.

"What did you do to Seraphina?" I asked the dragon after helping Astrid to her feet.

Everyone gathered behind Hodgepodge and me, forming a protective magical shield, even though the dragon still made no move to attack.

Stormwing heaved out a sigh as he lowered his wings and shook himself from snout to tail. "Why did you have to do that now?"

The strange dragon dipped its head.

Emberthorn grumbled a low note. "You may as well tell them."

"Tell us what?" Evander asked. "Have you been hiding another dragon all this time?"

"She's been hiding herself." Emberthorn lumbered over to the new arrival, leaving Stormwing to watch over Juniper and Cinder.

My gaze went to the burn marks on the forest floor where Seraphina had stood. The dragon was in the exact same spot. My gaze lifted to the dragon's placid face. "You're Seraphina?"

The dragon nodded. "I never meant to deceive you. But I couldn't tell you about my true form."

"You could! Bell has always been loyal to you." Hodgepodge stamped some more. "Why hide this from us?"

"I wasn't hiding anything from you specifically," Seraphina said. "And I've always been truthful about my dragon connection."

"No kidding, since you are one." Astrid brushed leaves off her clothes. "A heads-up before you went boom would have been appreciated."

Evander looked fascinated as he stared up at Seraphina. "It can't have been easy to conceal your form for so long. All that dragon magic stuffed into a tiny frame."

"It was her choice," Emberthorn said. "I never wanted this for Seraphina, but once I was trapped in stone, I could do little to guide her back to embracing who she was."

Seraphina's scales sparkled before the light died. "Emberthorn and Stormwing are my uncles. They're the family I wanted to impress, but nothing I did was good enough for them."

Stormwing growled. "Tell the truth."

Seraphina grumbled to herself. "I thought I wasn't good enough. And I thought I knew best. It felt like they held me back, stopped me from growing into my true power."

"So you taught them a lesson?" I asked. "You thought you'd find a new home with the Ithric family?"

"I was young, headstrong, and knew it all. I knew nothing. My uncles were looking out for me, making sure I didn't make too many errors as I grew into my power. But I was impatient, and I had a thirst for knowledge. I wanted to try everything at once."

"And there was nothing we could say or do to stop her," Stormwing said.

"You kept telling me to wait and not rush things. You said I'd make a mistake if I kept pushing too hard."

"Then you made a huge mistake," Evander said. "Trapping your uncles in stone will get you put in the naughty corner for the rest of your life."

I looked into Seraphina's eyes and saw nothing but sadness and regret. "It's a mistake she's been paying for ever since Emberthorn and Stormwing were captured. Seraphina has been devoted to bringing them back."

"The second they were captured, I realized my grave error," Seraphina said. "I didn't know what Lady Isolda planned to do to them."

Astrid snorted in disbelief. "You must have had some idea."

"No! She said they'd been polluted with dark power. And I wanted to believe that because they wouldn't let me do what I wanted. They were so strict."

"That's no excuse to behave like a brat," Astrid said.

"Which I understood when I saw what happened," Seraphina said. "After that, I couldn't trust Lady Isolda. She was behind all of it, despite Lord Crosby being in charge. He was her puppet and let her do whatever she liked."

"Probably because she was already addling his mind with toxic potions and magic," Hodgepodge said. He returned to my side, still glaring at Seraphina.

"Once Lady Isolda had trapped Emberthorn and Stormwing, did she come after you?" I asked.

"She said she wouldn't, but I knew she wouldn't be content with only capturing two dragons. I had to hide. So, I hid in this form. The castle's healer was about to retire, and I knew they'd be looking for a replacement. I showed up and filled the role."

Evander snorted a laugh. "All this time, Lady Isolda has had you under her roof, and she had no idea she housed a dragon."

"Seraphina isn't your real name, is it?" I asked.

"It's not, but I've used it for so long that I'll keep it. I had to change everything so I could work in the castle without causing suspicion. Lady Isolda found my interest in dragons amusing and let me gather books and resources, provided I did her bidding."

"That must have been a strain to keep the disguise in place," I said.

"Sometimes I wasn't successful," Seraphina said. "And since my uncles returned, it's grown harder to conceal my true form."

"Your itchy skin," I said. "That was the magic bond weakening?"

"And my form would shift without warning. I grew a tail in the castle and smashed up my room." Seraphina sighed. "I wanted to be back with my family, where I belonged. But I kept hiding what I really was because I didn't feel worthy of being a dragon."

"Until recently, I'd have agreed with you." Stormwing looked at Emberthorn and nodded.

"You've proven yourself worthy," Emberthorn said. "We would be honored if you'd fight with us."

Seraphina ducked her head again. "I've learned my lesson. I will always fight for my family. And sorry for transforming in front of you all. The disguise magic has been weakening for days. I felt it falling away and needed to be in the open so I didn't smash into any trees when I changed."

Juno and Hodgepodge didn't look happy, but other than a few bruises, no one had been harmed.

Evander clapped his hands together. "What are we waiting for? We have a castle to storm, prisoners to rescue, a wedding to prevent, and an unhinged ruler to dethrone."

"Sounds like a typical day to me." Astrid grabbed Evander by the shoulders, and they vanished in a flash of magic.

"We'll check the wedding preparations," Finn said.

Zandra scooped Juno up and settled her on her shoulder. She grabbed Finn's arm, Juno swirled out magic, and they also vanished.

I walked over to Seraphina, Hodgepodge my enormous shadow. "I missed the signs you were struggling."

"You missed nothing. You always asked what was troubling me. I wanted to tell you, but until I'd gotten my family free of the strife I caused, I couldn't risk dragging anyone else into my problems."

"We're dragged into the middle of them now," Hodgepodge said. "And Bell is at risk."

"I'm sorry for that," Seraphina said. "But I knew there was something special about Bell when we met. When you were younger, I'd watch you with your mother. She had a wonderful affinity with the dragons. She wasn't the right emissary for Emberthorn and Stormwing, but she would have suited another dragon perfectly."

"She could have worked with dragons?"

Seraphina nodded. "I was hopeful Clarice's abilities passed to you. The skills needed to be a successful dragon emissary are hard to find."

Now was the wrong time to ask, but I had to. "Lady Isolda said something about my mother being involved with Lord Crosby. Did you see anything like that?"

Seraphina shook her head. "Your mother was loyal and smart. Lord Crosby was a lazy fool. She was dedicated to two things: you and the dragons. No man would have turned her head."

"Not even my father," I murmured.

"She never gave up speaking out about the dragons," Seraphina said. "She even wrote articles about them. Lady Isolda hated her illegal publications. Clarice believed in the dragons as much as you do."

I was relieved Lady Isolda's poisoned words were false. My family was far from perfect, but we'd always loved each other. And now, I had another kind of family, and they needed help.

"I've felt different since I woke Emberthorn and Stormwing." I looked at the dragons. Juniper stood with Cinder. Stormwing stamped and huffed, impatient energy radiating off him. Emberthorn stood silently, watching me. He was waiting for me.

Hodgepodge turned his head and gazed down at me. "Well, lassie? Are we ready for one final fight?"

"It's time," I said. "We'll fly to the castle and see what's going on. Lady Isolda has insisted every villager attend Camilla's trial and the wedding, so the courtyard will be crowded. Everyone will see your arrival. She won't be able to hide behind her lies anymore."

Stormwing grumbled his approval. "Let's go snack on some royals."

# Chapter 19

I climbed on Hodgepodge's back and looked over my shoulders at the dragon army. No, my dragon army. I was their emissary, and it was my job to look out for them. But it was also my job to guide them. Dragons were ancient, rule-burdened creatures. An emissary's job was to ensure they didn't lose sight of what was important.

We were focused on one thing: get Emberthorn and Stormwing back where they belonged. Then, we'd end the Ithric family's tyrannical reign once and for all.

My fingers tingled with power as I conjured a spell I hadn't used for a long time. And I've never used it on so many large creatures.

"There's nothing to fear," Hodgepodge murmured. "Magic is like breathing."

Invisibility magic surged from my hands, rising in a pale pink mist. It floated over me and Hodgepodge and drifted behind us. It took less than a minute before we were all invisible.

"I did it," I whispered to Hodgepodge.

"I never doubted you for a second, lassie. Let's go deal with the rot in the castle." Hodgepodge crouched and inhaled.

"Problem?" I asked when we didn't move.

"If you're the emissary, what does that make me?"

"An irritating lizard," Stormwing muttered.

Hodgepodge hissed at him.

"You're my best friend," I whispered. "And I couldn't have done any of this without you."

He grunted then sprang. We were in the air, soaring over the treetops and away from the dragons' haven. Although my heart raced and my palms were sweaty, my mind was calm. We were doing the right thing. Change was hard, and sometimes it had to be forced, but the realm was long overdue for change. It had been trapped under the sharp spike of the Ithric family for too long. When people saw the dragons were back, everything would be different.

I held onto Hodgepodge's neck ruff as he blasted over the trees, his wings swishing as he glided on magic and air toward the castle. The only sign four other dragons accompanied me was the occasional flap of a heavy wing or a hot sulfury waft of breath skating past my ear.

"When we arrive, circle around the edge of the castle," I yelled. "We need to see what protection Lady Isolda has set up."

Hodgepodge surged onward, flying fast and straight, and within fifteen minutes, I spotted familiar turrets. He veered left and began a circuit of the castle's perimeter walls.

I wasn't surprised to see a heavy guard presence, but I was stunned to see the guards supported by wraiths chained at the castle's main entrance. They swirled and hissed as villagers scurried past and into the main courtyard that served as a public market, entertainment space, and location for trials and executions.

Hodgepodge flew lower, and I got a clear view of the courtyard. It was rammed full of people. Villagers weren't disobeying Lady Isolda by not showing up for the wedding. I suspected they'd be less keen to see the trial. Although Lady Isolda always proclaimed people had a right to see justice in action, people attended the public executions out of fear, not because they believed in her methods of punishment.

"We need to deal with those wraiths," Emberthorn said. "I doubt they'll be the only surprise Lady Isolda has in store for us, so the more problems we clear now, the better."

"She's not risking anything," I said. "Even if it means making a deal with those deviant creatures."

"There she is!" Stormwing said. "My next meal."

Lady Isolda ascended the wooden steps onto a raised platform at the back of the courtyard, accompanied by guards. She wore a glittering white gown, a fur-trimmed cape, and a sparkling tiara. She looked like she was getting married.

"The trial's about to begin," I said. "Look out for Evander and Astrid. If they've been successful, they should have gotten the others out of the dungeon, but they may need a quick escape."

We were too high to hear Lady Isolda, but I could tell she was speaking as she swept her arms around and prowled the raised platform, addressing the villagers.

Armed guards were stationed around the platform and at the edge of the courtyard. We were hugely outnumbered, but we had the element of surprise on our side.

A swirl of movement caught my attention. It was a fast-moving blur that shot into the air. It was Finn, rocketing into the sky in a blaze of white magic, his arms wrapped around two people.

Lady Isolda's screech was so loud even I heard it, and a second later, magic blazed, aimed at Finn. He twisted and twirled to avoid the strikes, but one wing was clipped, and he spiraled out of control.

I cried out in alarm as he plummeted, but a tornado of magic wrapped around him and tossed him into the air. Lady Isolda yelled orders, and more magic hailed down on the tornado, but it made no impact.

I squinted, not believing my eyes. Zandra was in the middle of the tornado. Her arms were out and her head tipped back as magic flooded out of her. Dancing around her feet, Juno flickered between her usual cat form and an ethereal creature, weaving spells and thrusting blasts of energy to sustain the tornado and protect her witch.

"Hodgepodge, are you seeing this?" I whispered.

"There's no avoiding it. They can handle themselves," he said. "And I think Finn has the bride and groom."

"From the way Lady Isolda is screaming, he's got something she needs."

"Release the wraiths!" Lady Isolda's voice boomed unnaturally loud.

Three wraiths zoomed toward the tornado. Juno thrust out a blast of impressive fire that slowed the wraiths, but they recovered and kept coming.

"Everyone else stay here," I ordered the dragons. "We'll bring the others back. Hodgie, let's go."

Hodgepodge moved lower, skirting the edge of the vast magical tornado. The wraiths, shadowy and formless, spiraled and dove.

Amid the airborne chaos, I spotted Zandra, Juno, and Finn surrounded by a swirl of malevolent shadows. Finn had his wings curled around Prince Jasper and his bride to be, while Zandra blasted out spell after spell, taking out wraiths. Juno sparkled and shimmered, a halo of magic protecting her and Zandra.

"Hodgepodge, let's scatter the wraiths!" I shouted over the rush of wind. With a determined roar, he banked sharply, sending us into a steep descent. I focused my energy, summoning bolts of crackling lightning that streaked toward the wraiths, disintegrating them upon impact.

The wraiths were cunning. They regrouped, their shadows intertwining to form a looming, malevolent figure. Fear gnawed at the edges of my resolve, but I pushed it aside. There was no room for hesitation.

"Dive!" I commanded, and Hodgepodge spiraled downwards, evading the dark entity. I called forth a whirlwind of fire, encircling our friends and incinerating the wraiths that dared approach.

Lady Isolda's enraged shrieks could still be heard. She couldn't see us under the cloak of magic, but she knew her enemy was here. And we weren't backing down.

Zandra's magic manifested in brilliant flashes of light, while Juno transformed into a swift and elusive form, darting between wraiths and taking them out with giant paw strikes.

We worked together, engaging the wraiths in a deadly dance and destroying their numbers. My spells crackled with power as I unleashed bursts of energy, dispersing the dark entities.

Outnumbered and defeated, the remaining wraiths spiraled in a shrieking circle before blasting away from the castle and abandoning Lady Isolda.

"You have impressive magic for such a small creature," Hodgepodge yelled at Juno. "Where does it come from?"

"Here and there," Juno said elusively, her gaze on us, even though she shouldn't have been able to see us. "And I'm older than I look, so I've picked up a few tricks over the decades."

"You looked different," Hodgepodge said. "You can shape-shift?"

"Can't we all?"

"Not without great effort."

Juno twitched her long white whiskers. "Finn caught the unhappy bride and groom. What should we do with them?"

"Climb on," I said. "Hodgepodge will take us to the others. Follow my voice."

"I see you just fine." Juno spiraled onto Zandra's shoulder as she hovered next to Finn. It was an impressive show of magic. "We'll follow you, so there's no need to burden your wyvern."

Hodgepodge snorted then turned and led us back to the others.

Out of sight of the castle courtyard, I removed the invisibility magic so everyone could be seen.

Finn dropped to the ground, unfurling his wings to reveal a startled Prince Jasper and a terrified Sophie, wearing a long, white wedding dress.

"What is going on?" Prince Jasper tumbled away from Finn and landed on his butt.

"We're saving you." Stormwing stamped a foot by his head. "But I'd be just as happy to eat you. You decide."

Seraphina snorted her surprise. "Careful. He could be valuable to us."

Prince Jasper's mouth hung open as he gaped at Stormwing. "You! You're... the dragon. The dead dragon."

"Not so dead anymore." I walked over to Sophie. "Are you injured?"

She shook her head, her eyes wide with shock as she took in the dragons. "This isn't part of the ceremony, is it?"

"No, but you're not safe in the castle. As you can see, our dragons are back, and they have questions for the family. Best if you stay out of it."

She nodded, too shocked to speak.

"What business is this of yours? I should—" Prince Jasper yelped as Cinder jumped on him and knocked him out.

"That's one way to deal with him," Seraphina said.

"The other is to eat him." Stormwing stamped again.

"We'll stay with Prince Jasper and Sophie and keep them safe," Juniper said. "As eager as Cinder is to fight, I won't risk her safety. She's too young for battle."

"Before we return, we'll bind them in so much magic, they'll barely be able to breathe," Juno said. "There'll be no risk to you or our baby."

"I want to fight!" Cinder flapped her wings as she jumped on Prince Jasper. "I don't want to stay and look after boring prisoners. The weak chinned one is no fun.

He's not even moving. And the one in the pretty dress is crying."

"Fighting is never fun," Juniper cautioned.

"I can't trust anyone else to do this," Juno said to Cinder. "Watch the prince and his almost bride carefully to ensure they don't escape. It's a very important job. It's a responsible job."

Cinder considered this option. "Since it's important, I'll do it." She grabbed Juno off Zandra's shoulder and flipped her into the air.

"Cinder! We've discussed you not dragon-handling without permission. And I need to talk to you about stamping on princes. Even if they are obnoxious." Juniper stomped over and intervened before Juno's fur got singed.

I turned to Finn. "You sit this next battle out, too. You got a battering when you went up against Lady Isolda."

He brushed soot off his wings and flapped them. "I've had worse. And I'm not letting you go back to that castle alone. And before you say anything, I know she's not alone, Hodgepodge, and I know you can whack me into next week with your tail, but we're stronger together. I'm standing with you."

"The dragons are out of the bag now," I said. "Lady Isolda knows the fight has come for her."

"Then what are we waiting for?" Finn asked.

I nodded. "Emberthorn and Stormwing. It's time to get you back on the throne."

# Chapter 20

I sat astride Hodgepodge as we flew back to the castle. This time, not cloaked under magic. Juno and Zandra rode Stormwing, while Finn rode Emberthorn. Seraphina took the rear position, watching for any wraiths that may reappear.

Although my heart beat frantically, I felt calmer than I had in a long time. When the villagers saw the dragons, Lady Isolda would have two options: accept the dragons or reveal herself as a traitor.

We'd decided on a simple approach to reveal Emberthorn and Stormwing. We'd fly down and circle the crowd. There'd be no way Lady Isolda could deny their existence with so many people watching. She'd have to get on board, or at least pretend she was. And with such a public return, there was less likely to be fighting or chaos.

"Is everybody ready?" I called out.

Emberthorn nodded, and Stormwing dipped a wing to show he'd heard me. Seraphina flicked her tail.

"We go in calmly. No theatrics."

"Was that aimed at me?" Stormwing asked. "And do theatrics mean I can't eat Lady Isolda?"

"We need to hear what she has to say when she's sees you're back," I said.

"Then I eat her?"

"Then we decide if she's going to trial or straight to jail," I said. "She has crimes to answer for."

"She'll deny everything," Emberthorn said.

"If she denies it too much, I'm definitely eating her," Stormwing said.

Emberthorn chuffed out a laugh. "I imagine she tastes of sour grapes. She'll be bitter to the core when she discovers her plan to destroy us failed."

"Watch out for any magic wards," I said. "Go in, calm and slow. People will get excited when they see you."

"They'll welcome us with open arms," Stormwing said.

"Some villagers will still be on the royal family's side," Emberthorn replied. "We must expect resistance and anger. Lady Isolda spread rumors that we'd abandoned the realm. We'll have questions to answer and trust to earn back."

"I'll direct them to their unworthy ruler." Stormwing grunted. "She'll get what's coming to her. I'll be picking her out of my teeth before sundown."

"Do you think there's any chance I'll stop him from eating Lady Isolda?" I whispered to Hodgepodge.

"Let him have his fun. He's earned it." Hodgepodge dipped lower. "The crowd is around the trial podium. Not many of them look happy, though."

"What could be joyful about seeing someone convicted for crimes they didn't commit?" I gripped Hodgepodge as we descended, going in slowly. Emberthorn and Stormwing flanked me on either side, Seraphina still behind us.

Hope and fear shoved through me like a fledgling dragon taking its first flight. This was it. As soon as we were spotted, there was no going back. The days of being an invisible person were over. After this, everyone would know my name.

We skimmed the turrets and circled overhead. By then, several villagers were looking up. They were shoving their friends and pointing. More people joined them, and soon all eyes were on us. But there was one particular set of eyes I was interested in. Lady Isolda stood on the wooden platform. She was barking orders, and guards were running in all directions.

"Have your shields ready." I cast a large protective circle of magic around Hodgepodge, ensuring his protection if the guards attacked.

Lady Isolda was gesturing and yelling so loud I could just hear her over Hodgepodge's wing flapping. By now, there was a row of guards along the outermost castle wall, magic blazing on their palms and their sparking magic staffs ignited. From their offensive positioning, Lady Isolda had given an order to attack.

"She won't go through with it," I murmured. "If her people see her attacking the dragons she's supposed to adore, it'll be game over for her."

"Perhaps she's too insane to care," Hodgepodge said.

A cheer rose from the crowd, growing in volume. People danced around and hugged each other. They were pointing at Emberthorn and Stormwing, blasting sparks of magic into the air. The magic wasn't a challenge or a threat. It was an expression of joy.

Lady Isolda must have sensed the mood shift. She stopped yelling orders and alternated between staring at us and glowering at the crowd. She made a signal with her hand, and the guards lowered their magic.

"That's the best welcome sign we're getting," Hodgepodge said. "I'm going in. Everyone, follow us."

I gestured at the others and took the lead. There was a landing site set aside for dragons. It was overgrown and dirty from disuse but would easily fit several full-sized dragons.

Hodgepodge landed first. Emberthorn next, Stormwing settled in beside him, and Seraphina landed behind them. They shook out their wings. Then Emberthorn tipped back his head and let out a groaning grumble that echoed off the castle walls and silenced the crowd. After a few seconds, Stormwing joined in, and then Seraphina.

Hodgepodge glanced at me and shrugged. "Should I bark-belch too? I'm not the same as them, but it sounds like fun."

"They're announcing themselves." The noise was otherworldly and beautiful, causing my heart to pound and tears to fill my eyes. The dragons were home.

Lady Isolda marched closer, surrounded by twenty heavily armed soldiers. Usually, her guards showed no expressions on their faces, but not this time. Most of them smiled, a few looked bemused, and one or two looked scared. It was the younger ones who seemed apprehensive about the dragons. It was possible they'd never met a dragon or had been young when Emberthorn and Stormwing were last here, and they'd forgotten what they looked like.

"What is the meaning of this?" Lady Isolda stopped a fair distance away from where we'd landed. "Who accompanies these beasts?"

I slid down Hodgepodge's side and partially concealed myself behind one of his large legs. I wanted to see how Lady Isolda would react to Emberthorn and Stormwing's return. Zandra, Juno, and Finn had also vanished the second we'd landed.

"Do you not remember us?" Emberthorn conducted a formal greeting, lowering his head in a show of respect Lady Isolda didn't deserve. Stormwing remained standing, and so did Seraphina.

Lady Isolda's face was a mask of contorted fury. "How are you here?"

"This realm needs our help," Emberthorn said. "We heard its cries and have come to aid you."

"No! You can't be here. You can't be trusted." She gestured at the watching villagers, their faces and gazes alive with happiness and surprise. "You betrayed us. You had to be stopped. How do I know I can trust you?"

"I could ask you the same question." Stormwing stamped a foot. "Tell the people what you did to us."

Lady Isolda's face soured with disgust. "I did what I had to do to protect my people. You were tainted with darkness, and a sickness overtook you. Everyone was at risk."

"Is that the truth?" Emberthorn murmured.

"Of course! And we all thought you were dead."

"We're a lot harder to kill than some might believe. Stone may trap, but it doesn't always kill." Stormwing stamped again. "The talk of darkness was a lie from your household, so you would succeed in your greedy desire to control everything."

There was murmuring among the villagers, but no one spoke up to defend this idea.

Lady Isolda's expression froze. She was digging her fingers into the tops of her arms. "I must have misheard you. You're accusing my precious, loyal family of something unjust? After everything we have done to keep the realm surviving. Ever since your cankerous cruelty disrupted things, it's been a struggle."

"I'm stating facts," Stormwing said. "We were never sick or troubled with dark magic. You manipulated a family member into helping trap us. You thought you were so clever."

Lady Isolda shook her head, her expression a mask of righteousness. "Everything I do is for the good of my people."

"Lies! If you'd been smart, you'd have smashed every dragon bone you possessed rather than greedily hoarding them while you figured out how to use our ancient power for yourself." A plume of hot smoke shot from Stormwing.

"This is ridiculous. You may look like the dragons that ruled here, but you can't be them," Lady Isolda said. "This is fraud. We must stop them."

None of her guards moved, and no one in the crowd joined in with cries of support for Lady Isolda.

"Take these imposters away!" she commanded. "I will interrogate them and learn the true meaning of this deceit."

Several soldiers stepped forward, but the majority remained where they were.

Lady Isolda grabbed two staffs from her guards' hands, slammed them into the ground, and pointed them at Stormwing. A jagged crackle of magic shot toward him.

He responded with a huge blast of fire, searing the air and sucking away the oxygen. It bounced off a protective shield around Lady Isolda and her guards, leaving them unharmed.

"You see! They're not here to help," she screeched. "These things are unnatural. They were polluted years ago. Someone is controlling them. I demand to know who is with that other creature. I saw you when you landed!" Lady Isolda pointed at Hodgepodge.

Hodgepodge swiped his tail through the air and puffed out smoke.

While Lady Isolda continued screeching and barking orders, summoning more soldiers to surround her so she'd be protected from any magic, I drew in a deep breath and pulled back my shoulders.

"You don't have to do this," Hodgepodge cautioned. "The dragons are back. You've done enough."

"I'm their emissary. It's my job to negotiate peace or minimize the damage if we can't find a solution." I pressed a kiss to his leg and stepped in front of him. Immediately, I was flanked by Finn, Zandra, and Juno.

Juno caught my eye and nodded. "We've dealt with worse than this screeching monster. If you require her to be obliterated, just say the word."

"Juno loves to obliterate." Zandra's expression was set to stern. "We've got your back. Whatever you need from us, we're here."

Finn nodded, his expression full of confidence as his wings fluttered.

I took a few steps forward but was stopped by Hodgepodge, curling his tail around my feet.

"That's close enough to the real monster," he muttered.

"Who are you?" Lady Isolda asked. "Wait! I know you."

"I'm the dragons' emissary," I said.

"No, you're not." Lady Isolda brushed the guards aside as she drew closer. "You're that cleaner, the one meddling in Camilla's life. You have no power here."

"She does," Emberthorn said. "Bell is linked to us. She is our emissary and therefore has our power. She also has her own strong magic. You'd be wise to listen to what she has to say. She speaks for us. Bell advises us. She also set us free."

"You really have lost your mind if you put a common servant in charge of your destiny." Lady Isolda's top lip curled.

But she no longer intimidated me. I saw through the smoke and shadows to the monster inside the gowns and jewels. Lady Isolda cared only about herself and the power she could amass. She'd almost ruined this realm in her single-minded desire to take everything she wanted. Today, that ended.

"I speak for the dragons," I said. "And I hope I speak for everyone here when I say we want them back. Darkness never tainted Emberthorn and Stormwing. Lady Isolda discovered they had a weakness and used it against them. She turned another dragon to her ways and trapped Emberthorn and Stormwing. All these years, the statues you've visited in the chamber were their prison."

The crowd collectively gasped.

"Don't listen to this peasant," Lady Isolda spat out. "She's discovered a false moment of glory and is grasping at it with her filthy hands. No one cares about your voice or your opinion. You are nothing."

"I do," someone called from the crowd. "Bell's good to me."

"Same here," someone else yelled out. "She's always got a kind word and a moment to share, no matter how busy she is."

"She's got a heart of gold."

My cheeks heated as more people called out what they thought of me. All this time, I'd thought I was invisible, that no one cared about me or noticed me. But they did. And they were all listening to what I had to say. They believed me.

I drew strength from their solidarity and met Lady Isolda's fierce glare head-on. "Are you prepared to rule with the dragons again, after paying for your crimes?"

"I've had enough!" Lady Isolda said. "Guards, surround the dragons. This dark witch has corrupted them. They left us. They don't deserve to return to this realm."

None of the guards moved.

"I'm a dark witch now?" I asked. "A moment ago, you thought me a powerless servant, not fit to scrape the mud from your boots."

Lady Isolda twisted to face her guards. "I gave an order, and I insist you carry it out."

The guards remained resolute, although several shifted uncomfortably, as if they were considering breaking rank.

"Warwick! Warwick! Where are you? Control your soldiers," Lady Isolda screamed.

Wherever Warwick was hiding, he had no plan to assist Lady Isolda. I hoped he stayed out of sight. If she realized he was involved, she'd destroy him.

"I'll ask again," I said calmly. "If you accept you've done wrong and pay for your crimes, there's an opportunity for you to rule alongside each other. Emberthorn and Stormwing will forgive you."

"We will?" Stormwing grumbled.

"I can't trust those things! Just as I cannot trust you," Lady Isolda said. "I should have known you were behind this. You were always there, meddling in our lives. You're the reason Camilla's lost her mind and been attempting to murder my son. And what have you done with Jasper? Given him to your dragon pets?"

"Camilla is innocent. You have no right to hold her." My gaze flickered to movement at the back of the crowd, and I was happy to see Evander and Astrid leading Camilla, Valerie, and Griffin to safety.

"Oh! This makes sense now." Lady Isolda clasped her hands together. "All this time, I've never noticed you. You must have powerful magic to ensure you could weave your evil ways through the castle without me uncovering your twisted plan."

"Bell is full of goodness," Emberthorn said. "That's why she was invisible to you. You lost your kindness a long time ago in the pursuit of more and more power. It was your undoing."

Lady Isolda cackled a laugh and flipped a hand in the air. "Perhaps I've made a few mistakes, but I did my best."

"You'll admit you've done wrong?" I asked.

She smirked. "I recognize it's time to stand aside and let someone else rule."

"You want the dragons to rule without you?" I didn't like the sharp look in her eyes.

Lady Isolda speared me with a filthy glare. "Oh, no. But I am prepared to stand aside for my heir. I'm interested to know what he'll do about this woeful situation."

"Prince Jasper will need support," I said. "He could do a lot worse than have dragons as co-rulers."

"Not that fool." Lady Isolda raised her hands above her head, and sparks of magic cascaded around her. "Come to me. I summon you."

The crowd hurriedly parted as something charged through them, knocking people over. I couldn't see what it was since there were so many villagers crammed into the space, but a foul, charred smell filled the air and made my eyes water.

"What in the name of all things unholy dragon is that?" Finn muttered as he peered over people's heads.

My breath left me as an ungodly roar ripped through the air, and a broken, pieced-together Prince Godric charged at me.

# Chapter 21

Shock ricocheted to my bone marrow, and if it hadn't been for Hodgepodge sweeping me off my feet and batting Prince Godric back with his tail, I wouldn't have been in one piece. Prince Godric had moved so quickly that his stone encased arm had brushed against my face, hot sparks of magic pinging against me.

I scrambled to my feet, my eyes wide, and my hands held out as Prince Godric roared his rage once again. The sound was broken and hoarse, and his gaze held nothing but hatred. And that hatred was aimed at me.

"What is that thing?" Finn yelled.

"Prince Godric. Lady Isolda's son." Although I recognized him, his handsome arrogance was mismatched and held together by flares of magic that slid between the cracks in his stone skin.

"Take our revenge, my son," Lady Isolda shouted. "This witch stands in your way of taking control. There has always been a troubling energy in our castle, and I've discovered its source. Destroy her, and we'll have all the riches. You'll get your place by my side."

Stormwing blasted fire at Prince Godric, but it bounced off him, and the stone prince barely noticed he was engulfed in a haze of powerful dragon flame. Whatever Lady Isolda had used to bring Prince Godric back was forged from old, dark, forbidden magic. Maybe magic that was older than the dragons themselves.

Lady Isolda responded with ferocity, but rather than attacking Stormwing, she lobbed a crackle of dark energy into the crowd. "You're making me punish my subjects. If any of them die, it will be your fault. If you care for this realm, save your people."

"She's as crazy as her son," Emberthorn grumbled.

"Don't listen to the dragons," Lady Isolda screeched, pouring more magic over the scattering, screaming crowd. "They've ruined this realm by abandoning us. And now they're back to take the scraps and leave us to die."

"Stop! These people have done nothing wrong to you," I yelled. "They're not your enemy. Juno, Finn, Zandra, protect them."

Finn took to the air while Zandra and Juno swirled away in a magical blast, channeling people to safety while rebuffing Lady Isolda's magic.

"Why is she still talking?" Lady Isolda glowered at Prince Godric as she pointed at me. "You have your orders. Destroy the dragon witch."

Although most of the crowd was being led to safety by my friends, several remained standing. And they weren't scared. They looked angry. And that anger was directed at Lady Isolda.

"Leave Bell alone." It was Gwit Buckleberry and his sister, Maggie. They held magic that flared protectively around them.

I shook my head and gestured for them to go. They put themselves at too much risk by protecting me. But they weren't alone. Many of the women we'd rescued from the ship stood strong, too. And another dozen villagers joined them. Between them, they raised an enormous barrier of magic against the onslaught Lady Isolda tossed at the crowd, keeping the stragglers safe from harm.

"Can't you see what she's making you do? You're breaking the realm's rules. You shouldn't use magic against me," Lady Isolda bellowed. "Bell has revealed herself as a servant to the dragons, and their corruption has twisted her. If my son doesn't kill her, we'll be ruined."

That son could barely hold his form together, as Lady Isolda was distracted by her subjects standing against her. But he was fast and had been dodging Hodgepodge's tail ever since he'd revealed himself. Chunks fell off Prince Godric every time he landed on the ground or got hit by Hodgepodge. Prince Godric was literally falling apart.

Lady Isolda swirled toward her guards as her spells bounced off the villagers' protective magic. "I will give you one last order. If any of you disobey, you'll be killed on the spot."

"Join us," I called out to them, ensuring I kept a safe distance from Prince Godric as he raged and roared, still held back by my wonderful wyvern. "Things must change. We can't keep living like this. Everyone is scared, and our magic is repressed. Remember how life was with the dragons. We can be free and happy again."

Lady Isolda tipped back her head, and a harsh, vicious scream flooded the courtyard. The remaining villagers fell to the ground, covering their ears. The hesitant guards swayed side to side and collapsed. My ears rang with the unnatural sound that darkened my thoughts, and when I touched my top lip, I found it bloody.

"If I want something done properly, I must do it myself." Lady Isolda lifted her hands above her head and screamed again.

The courtyard erupted into chaos as she unleashed a torrent of vicious magic upon Hodgepodge, Seraphina, Emberthorn, and Stormwing.

My heart raced at the ferocity of her attack as spells crackled, each one aimed at the dragons.

I sprinted toward Hodgepodge, stumbling on the uneven ground. His gaze met mine after he'd swiped Prince Godric away with a giant wing, his eyes reflecting worry and determination.

"Protect them!" I shouted, my voice drowned by the roars and thunder of Lady Isolda's assault.

Emberthorn, Stormwing, and Seraphina twisted and turned, their scales ablaze with magic and fire, evading the relentless barrage. Lady Isolda was fast, her movements fueled by rage and dark power. Her spells struck like lightning, finding their marks with deadly accuracy.

Emberthorn's wing was twisted, a trail of smoke rising from the injured membrane. Stormwing's side bore the brunt of a dark spell, and his scales glowed with an unnatural, sickly hue. My heart clenched at the sight of their pain.

Seraphina fought bravely, using her body as a barrier to protect her family. But it wasn't enough. Lady Isolda was determined to destroy and burn through every spell she had in her arsenal to ensure victory.

Hodgepodge positioned himself between me and the dragons, creating another barrier with his massive wings. I summoned every ounce of magic within me, forming another shield around us. The dragons needed time to recover.

Lady Isolda's eyes gleamed with madness as she launched another assault, and her spells blasted through my magic. Stormwing staggered, and Emberthorn's movements grew labored.

My mind raced, searching for a solution amidst the turmoil. I darted toward Emberthorn, my hands glowing with healing magic. The dragons needed strength, and I could give it to them. We shared magic now, so they could have mine.

I touched his scales, and warmth surged through my fingertips. Emberthorn's eyes, dulled with pain, flickered with a renewed vigor. I turned to Stormwing and did the same. He roared defiantly, shaking off the lingering effects of Lady Isolda's dark spells, and they faced her. Fire danced in their eyes, and a tempest brewed in the air.

Seraphina waved me away with one wing. "Don't give us everything. You need some to protect yourself and Hodgepodge."

Lady Isolda hesitated as she summoned more magic, her arrogance faltering as the dragons rose again. It was the fraction of a second they needed. Emberthorn unleashed a torrent of searing flames, while Stormwing conjured smoke that whipped Lady Isolda off her feet.

She crashed down, her dark magic scattering across the stone. The spell slammed into Hodgepodge, and he dropped to the ground, magic crackling across him and pinning him. He was unable to move.

"Stop this madness," I urged, my voice cutting through the tension as my gaze settled on Hodgepodge. "We can find a way to heal the wounds you've caused."

Lady Isolda's laugh was bitter. "You know nothing of what I've endured. This realm will be mine, or it will crumble to ashes."

With a shared roar that echoed through the courtyard, Emberthorn and Stormwing unleashed their combined magic, creating a vortex of fire that enveloped Lady Isolda. It seared the air, forcing me to look away, the flames were so hot and bright.

The fire was joined by a blast of intense white magic and a swirl of rainbow glitter as Finn, Juno, and Zandra added their magic from the other side of the courtyard.

With Lady Isolda contained, I backed away and ran to Hodgepodge. His breathing was labored, and he had a deep wound on his side. His left front leg wasn't moving.

He grunted and wheezed out a breath. "I hate quests."

"This one is almost over. Let me heal you."

He shook his head. "I'll live. Where's Prince Godric? I broke him the last time I hit him with my tail, but I don't see him now."

"I think he's gone." I checked Hodgepodge over, brushing off Lady Isolda's magic as best I could, although it was sticky and stank of disease.

"And Lady Isolda?"

I glanced up. As Emberthorn and Stormwing's flames subsided, the courtyard grew quiet.

Lady Isolda had vanished.

Emberthorn and Stormwing exchanged glances, their keen eyes searching for any sign of her.

"Is she gone for good?" I asked, my hand resting on Hodgepodge's head.

Emberthorn's gaze softened as he shook his head. Stormwing, too, seemed unsure, his wings twitching with a residual tension.

"Magic of that caliber is hard to destroy. She might have vanished or..."

"Or she perished," Stormwing finished the thought, his eyes scanning the space Lady Isolda had stood. "Let's hope that's true. I'm disappointed I never got to eat her."

The villagers, cautiously emerging from their hiding places, mirrored our uncertainty, still protected by Finn, Juno, and Zandra.

"Bell, look out!" Seraphina cried.

Prince Godric leapt over Hodgepodge and landed in front of me, the ground shuddering under the impact. The chunks of stone protecting him were gone. He was held together by a mix of smoke and shadow that swirled and eddied every time he took a grating breath. He grabbed for me, but I dodged away and blasted him with a spell.

I backed up, leading him away from an injured Hodgepodge. "Let me help. You're under your mother's spell. She had no right to bring you back. You must be in pain."

Prince Godric snarled and swung a wild punch at me.

"Your mother never wanted to step aside and let you rule. Can't you see how wrong all of this is?"

He slammed a fist into the ground. He held out his palm, and a flickering ball of amber light emerged.

I raised a protective shield and braced myself for the impact.

Prince Godric was hit from above. He flew off his feet and slammed into the dirt.

My gaze shot to the turrets. Grand Dame Ravenswood was perched on the edge of her turret, her hair blowing free, as she held aloft her arms. She fired on Prince Godric several more times, pinning him and saving me.

I was unsure if she realized who she was attacking, but I was grateful for the reprieve.

The temperature dropped, and I turned, foreboding rubbing a sharp blade across my spine. Something was coming.

Black ice crackled across the courtyard, encasing everything it touched and causing the villagers to flee again. Lady Isolda surged out of the ground and shot into the air on a pillar of ice. She flung out a spell that encased her remaining soldiers and Prince Godric, forcing them to their feet.

"My orders still stand. Guards, destroy the dragons. Godric, why is Bell still standing? Kill her." Purple veins pulsed beneath her skin, and her eyes glinted black.

The soldiers lumbered toward the dragons, their movements jagged and reluctant, and their faces showing horror at being forced to perform for Lady Isolda. She held her hands out, magic blazing over the guards to ensure they did her bidding.

The ground shook as Prince Godric lumbered toward me. He lifted a hand and made a fist. An iron-like grip encased my throat, and I couldn't breathe. I struggled against the fierce magic, my feet dragging through the dirt as he drew me nearer, a gurgling growl of torment slipping from his mouth.

Emberthorn, Stormwing, and Seraphina roared their rage as the guards engulfed them in a barrage of magic. Finn, Juno, and Zandra joined them, putting themselves between the dragons and Hodgepodge as they blasted magic.

I was on my own with Prince Godric. But I'd stopped him before, and I could do it again. This time, it would be for good.

Lady Isolda screeched, drawing my attention. She was being attacked by Lord Frederick. The ghost twirled her around, alternating between knocking her off balance and blasting through her magic, disconnecting her from the soldiers doing battle with the dragons and giving them a chance to fire back.

Lord Frederick caught my eye and cackled a laugh before shooting straight through Lady Isolda.

I'd never been more grateful to have so many allies. It gave me time to focus. Even though my throat burned, I forced myself to relax.

A flash of recognition flickered in Prince Godric's eyes as I came to within touching distance of him, though I was uncertain if he knew me. The magic he'd been forced to endure must have broken his body and mind.

The pain lessened, and I could breathe again. I drew in a shaky breath, and we looked at each other. The prince against the servant. It shouldn't have been a match, but I believed in myself. I believed in this cause and this realm, and I'd always promised I'd do anything to get the dragons back. It was time to prove that.

Prince Godric staggered as a spell from Lady Isolda slammed into him. He growled, and his attention turned to his mother, who was still doing battle with Lord Frederick while keeping a tenuous hold on her warring soldiers.

Prince Godric tipped back his head and howled, his rage rearing up, and he turned back to me with a snarl.

I thrust out a spell that froze him in place. Then approached slowly. "You've done this realm a great wrong, but I know this final battle isn't your fault. I don't want to destroy you, but if you remain free, you'll be a threat to the dragons. I'm their emissary. I speak for them, and I protect them."

Prince Godric shook as he fought against my spell, but it held.

"If I let you live, you'll always hurt them. And you'll always want to hurt me, Hodgepodge, and my friends. I can't allow that to happen."

A shudder ran through him as Lady Isolda's magic slammed into him again. But rather than responding violently, he closed his eyes and sighed. When he opened them, they were the clear beautiful blue they'd always been. "Please, release me."

I could have taken his words to mean several things, but I chose to believe he knew he'd gone too far. The stone heart amulet had broken him, and while his mother pieced him together, she'd done it for the wrong reasons. She didn't want her son back because she loved him and wanted to nurture this realm with him by her side. While Lady Isolda's dark magic fueled Prince Godric, he would only ever do harm.

I conjured a spell, placed my hands on Prince Godric's shoulders, and whispered a goodbye. He shattered, turning to dust.

Lady Isolda screamed again when she saw he was gone. She'd lost, and she knew it. Although the soldiers were still fighting, their forced magic was no match for the dragons or my powerful friends. Lady Isolda hissed and fled skyward, leaving behind a streak of grey smoke and cracking black ice.

"No, you don't. I've been waiting for this meal for a long time." Stormwing leaped, grabbed Lady Isolda in his mouth, landed, swallowed, and then burped.

We all stared at him.

Hodgepodge chuffed out a laugh. "Best place for her."

The guards, released from Lady Isolda's spell, stopped attacking and stood, looking confused.

"Juno. Zandra. Watch the guards. They'll have questions. Finn, find Evander and Astrid. Make sure no one is injured and everyone got out of the dungeon in one piece." I raced over to Hodgepodge and wrapped my arms around his neck. "Are you doing good?"

"No. And I still hate foolhardy, dangerous quests." He was bleeding, but the wound would heal.

"Brother, we spoke about this." Emberthorn lumbered over to Stormwing. "Lady Isolda must pay for her crimes. If you digest her, she won't be able to stand trial."

"This is her punishment. Although you were right, she tastes foul." Stormwing burped again. "Like rotten cherries and gremlin gas."

"Cough her up." Emberthorn thumped Stormwing with his tail. "You swallowed her whole, so she's still alive."

I remained by Hodgepodge, too exhausted to argue with Stormwing over his recent choice of meal.

"Don't be stubborn," Emberthorn said. "Our emissary doesn't approve."

"Bell thinks eating Lady Isolda is an excellent idea," Stormwing said.

"It's an understandable thing to want to do," I said, "but I agree with Emberthorn. Lady Isolda stripped this realm of everything, including the dragons. And although some may see her being eaten by a dragon as a suitable punishment, there'll be others who'll have many questions and will want to see her fairly tried and justice done."

"You're too sensible to work with us," Stormwing said.

"Which makes her our perfect emissary," Emberthorn said. "Between your hotheadedness and my occasional lapse into laziness, Bell is the perfect go-between."

Stormwing huffed and puffed before giving a hacking cough and spitting Lady Isolda out. She was unconscious but alive, although covered in sticky dragon spit.

Seraphina pinned her under a large clawed foot. "She's going nowhere."

Hodgepodge heaved out a sigh. "Now that's over, it's time to have a nice piece of blueberry pie and a nap."

# Chapter 22

"We're due to meet Evander in fifteen minutes." Hodgepodge was perched on my shoulder, snuffling in my ear as I stood in the castle courtyard. The quiet, peaceful courtyard with no surly guard presence or air of intimidation that made people scuttle about with their heads down.

"I haven't forgotten, but I want to see what will happen."

"Are you worried Camilla will stay?"

"No! She was grateful to be rescued from the dungeon, but she's happy to leave and never see this place again," I said. "But I wondered if she'd linger longer than necessary. Camilla has always been kind to her sister."

Three days had passed since the realm was tipped on its head and violently shaken. Everything had changed. Or rather, everything was just the way it should be. Emberthorn and Stormwing were accepted back as rulers. No one from the Ithric family was involved. Lord Crosby and Grand Dame Ravenswood had been released from their prison turrets and were receiving medical treatment under Seraphina's close attention.

If they were free of all dark magic malevolence, negotiations would take place to see if they wanted a return to rule. For now, it was just the dragons in charge.

When those negotiations started, I'd be a key part of them. And although those matters should have my full attention, there was a small happily-ever-after I was determined to see take place before Camilla and Valerie returned home.

"Bell, we need to move." Hodgepodge hopped up and down. "I want to see what Evander's surprise is."

"Knowing him, it could be anything," I said.

"He said it'll change our lives. Maybe he's bought a pie factory. We'll get custom-made blueberry pies whenever we want. Imagine that!"

I chuckled and patted his side. Hodgepodge was fully healed after the fight. Seraphina may be back in her dragon form, but she was still a skilled healer and had wasted no time in ensuring everyone recovered from their battle injuries.

"Look! There they are," I said.

Camilla and Valerie emerged from the castle, followed a few seconds later by several assistants who piled bags and belongings into the waiting carriage.

I grinned as Griffin appeared. He was smartly dressed and looking handsome as he spoke to Valerie. After a moment of conversation, she kissed his cheek before climbing into the carriage with Camilla, who looked on with amusement and fondness.

"I knew he had the courage to do it," I murmured.

"He'll have his hands full if he gets involved with that family," Hodgepodge said.

"Valerie's the calm sister. And although Camilla is eccentric, she did nothing wrong. She found herself in an awful situation and let her imagination run wild."

"She dreamed up a hundred ways to murder Prince Jasper," Hodgepodge said. "I pity Griffin if he gets on the wrong side of Valerie."

"We'll keep an eye on the relationship and make sure it goes smoothly." I hailed Griffin, and he walked over, glancing over his shoulder as the carriage moved away. "Did they get off safely?"

He nodded. "I wanted to make sure they didn't run into any difficulties on their way out. People are still twitchy after everything that happened."

"It's what I'd expect from such a kindhearted man," I said. "Valerie is sweet."

Griffin blushed. "She is. I... I like her."

"When are you planning to visit?"

He couldn't hide his smile. "Two weeks. Camilla promised to talk incessantly about how wonderful I am, so their parents will welcome me. I just hope they're impressed by someone who works in the stables."

"Anyone who makes their daughter smile like you do Valerie is worthy," I said. "And perhaps the dragons will have a new role for you, if you're looking for an impressive title to wow your future in-laws."

Griffin shrugged. "I like the horses. I don't want to go back to soldiering. Maybe I could ride them more than muck them out, though."

"The dragons will find you a job you enjoy," I said. "Are you joining us to see what Evander has planned?"

"I have no choice. He insisted everyone be there. Have you any idea what he's up to?" Griffin fell into step with us as we headed out of the castle courtyard.

"Not a clue. Although Astrid is in on it, too. She kept smirking and laughing to herself when Evander was telling us where to go."

"Those two are trouble when they're together," Griffin said. "What about Warwick?"

"What about me?" Warwick appeared from the shadows, one arm heavily strapped, and his face a painful looking bloom of bruises, even after receiving hours of magical healing.

"You're joining us too?" I'd barely seen him since the battle. Lady Isolda had attacked him and left him for dead. He'd been lucky to survive.

"There's not much else for me to do." Warwick walked alongside me, favoring one leg as he tried to hide a limp. "My soldiers are still receiving treatment. I've given them all a week off. They need to rest, and so do I. Having spent so long deceiving Lady Isolda, I'm overdue a vacation."

"You deserve it. Any news on your new dungeon guests?" I asked.

Warwick squinted as the sun shone in his eyes. "Prince Jasper is feigning ignorance. He's blaming everything on his mother."

"They're as bad as each other," Hodgepodge said. "Get rid of them both. I still can't understand why Emberthorn made Stormwing spit up Lady Isolda."

"Because she has a list of crimes to answer for," Warwick said. "She's talking. Well, in a way. She screams when I question her and keeps telling me she wishes she had killed me, but she knows she's defeated. Her confession is slowly coming out. And Prince Jasper was rattled when he learned what happened to his brother. He didn't know what Lady Isolda had done to him. That news could be enough to get him to turn against her. He's already hinted that he knows she's behind the curse, stopping anyone getting pregnant."

"Curse us all and blame it on the dragons," Hodgepodge muttered.

"Prince Jasper thinks he can make a deal with the information," Warwick said. "He can try. It might save his life, but he won't ever see freedom."

"Their rule is over," I said. "And we're in safe hands now. Emberthorn and Stormwing will work tirelessly to restore the realm."

"And if either of them gets too lazy or bossy, you'll put them in their place." Hodgepodge sighed. "I have a feeling our quiet nights by a warm hearth with a big piece of pie have become a distant memory."

"We'll make time to relax," I said. "And there'll always be time for pie. How about Sophie?"

"Returned home. She was glad to escape with her life," Warwick said.

We walked along the busy main road, away from the castle. The air felt different. Magic was free again, and although people were hesitant about using it, there was a familiar frisson of energy that had once permeated this village. Villagers were regaining their confidence in using spells, potions, and charms. And everything was responding positively to magic's return. The sun was shining, and the air was warm and sweetly scented. It would take time, but we'd rebuild what we'd lost.

"Do you know where we're going?" I asked Warwick.

"I have an idea."

"Care to share?"

He shook his head. "It's better if you see for yourself."

"See what?" Hodgepodge asked. "There'll be no more quests. If Evander plans on dragging us somewhere because he has a dumb adventure planned, I'll bite him. Our adventuring days are over."

"It's an adventure of sorts," Warwick said. "But for it to work, it needs careful planning. It's not the dumbest idea he's ever had. I don't hate it."

I increased my pace, eager to discover what Evander and Astrid had brewed up between them. They were adventurers to the core, so I could only imagine it meant something dangerous with big stakes and a high chance of failure.

"We need to go through the portal tunnel." Warwick directed as through the village.

"Are we traveling far?" I didn't like to be away from the dragons. Although they were busy getting into their routine and introducing Juniper and Cinder to their new home, they needed time to fully recover and make plans for the realm now they ruled alone.

"Those hulking great beasts will be fine without you mollycoddling them," Warwick said. "I'll go first. Hold on to me, so you don't get lost."

I stood between Warwick and Griffin. Warwick pressed his hand against the stone, whispered a few words, and we were whisked to a lush, green forest. The air was warm and alive with birdsong. It was a sound I hadn't heard for a long time. I closed my eyes and breathed in deeply, enjoying the feel of the sun on my face and the sweet sounds.

"Is this it?" Hodgepodge sounded unimpressed. "I thought we'd be getting fed."

"We had breakfast two hours ago," I said. "You can't be hungry already."

"It's the shape-changing," he said. "It burns through the calories."

"You've not gone large since Seraphina healed you."

"I had a small breakfast."

"There they are!" Evander strode past a bank of fir trees, Astrid by his side. "Let me show you around."

"What are you showing us?" I asked. "And where is this?"

"Where doesn't matter. Although we're still inside the realm." Evander slung an arm around my shoulders. "It's an easy trip through the portal tunnel, and this is the perfect location for our new base."

"Base for what?" Hodgepodge asked, standing tall on my shoulder as he peered around.

"A base for all of us. This way." Evander led us along a path of trodden grass and out of the trees. Emberthorn, Stormwing, Juniper, and Cinder stood in a large clearing.

"I thought you were at the castle," I said. "You're in on this too?"

"Bell, relax. There's no great conspiracy against you." Astrid's smile was wry. "After everything you did for us, we got to thinking about how we could repay you."

"This was my idea," Evander said.

"I thought of it first." Astrid shoved him.

"You don't have to repay me. But I'm intrigued. Tell me more." I formally greeted the dragons, who lounged in the long grass, although Cinder occasionally jumped up and down on Stormwing's back.

Finn, Juno, and Zandra emerged from behind Stormwing.

"Greetings!" Juno said. "We thought we'd join in the celebrations before returning to Crimson Cove."

"For the love of all things dragon! Why are we here, and what are we celebrating?" I was careful not to stare at Finn. That angel got more handsome every day.

"Bell, you need an upgrade." Emberthorn rolled to his feet and shook himself from snout to tail. "Your home is charming, but it's not appropriate for our emissary."

"It's a damp hovel," Stormwing said. "It smells of smoke, and when I peeked through the window, I saw a mouse on the counter."

"It's not that bad. It can get cold, but it's suited me for years. And Hodgepodge chases away the mice."

"You've put up with it for years," Emberthorn said. "There's a difference. You don't have to now. We considered offering you a castle turret as your new home, but given the dark deeds Lady Isolda has undertaken within those walls, it's not appropriate. The stones need to be cleansed to remove the foul stench of malevolence."

"Live in the castle?" I shook my head. "I don't want that. But I've got ideas for brightening the place up."

"I'll listen to those ideas," Emberthorn said. "But we wanted something new for you. Then Evander told us about his land."

"You have land?" I asked Evander.

He shrugged. "I needed somewhere to invest my ill-gotten gains. Lady Isolda wanted to buy this area and cut down the trees. She had plans to build an enchanted creature zoo to impress visiting nobles. It sounded nasty. Anyway, I pretended I was someone important and wanted to mine the land for precious stones. Anything I found, we'd split the profits. She sold it to me for an over-inflated price, but I couldn't let her ruin this paradise. I've been coming here since I was a kid. It means something to me."

"Such a softhearted dolt," Astrid said.

Evander grinned good-naturedly. "It's mine now. And I'm gifting it to everyone. We're setting up our own version of Wild Wing in the realm. It'll be a place for dragons to rest and spend time together. People can make connections with dragons who visit from anywhere in the world and form alliances. Maybe even start a dragon rider school."

I looked around the clearing. "That'll take a huge amount of work. Wild Wing is unique."

"It is a special place," Emberthorn said. "But we need more places like that. A safe space for all magic users. And we have plenty of talking to do with other dragons. There's much work to undertake to fully repair this realm. And we can't do it alone."

"You're not alone." Seraphina emerged from the trees in her dragon form. She hadn't shifted since she exploded into her scales and flame. "We have each other. And with Bell as our emissary, we'll always be steered correctly. I've met no one with a purer heart."

I was still getting used to Seraphina's magnificent new form, but her voice was the same. I formally greeted her. "That's kind of you to say."

"I speak the truth. We don't want the castle taint to ruin our plans. I thought we could turn the castle into a grand museum. Or housing for those less fortunate. We need a fresh start, with fresh ideas." Seraphina bowed her head. "But only if you think the idea has wings."

"It won't happen overnight," Evander said, "but I want to build houses for all of us here and to ensure there's plenty of room for dragons to feel at home. Roosting places, secure caves, dens for new mothers. Anything they like. I've been talking to Juniper about designs, and we've gotten so many ideas."

"Does this mean you're giving up your lifetime of misdeeds to become a property developer?" I asked.

"Don't bet on that," Astrid said. "We need funds to ensure this magic happens. You should hear some of Evander's crazier plans. It'll cost a fortune."

"And to get that fortune, I fully intend to steal, rob, and plunder anyone who has a bad word to say about the dragons. But all of that money will be invested here." A shiver of uncertainty crossed Evander's face as he focused on me. "What do you think, Bell? Would you like this to be your new home, too?"

It took me a moment before the enormity of the offer sank in. I'd worked hard to be happy with what little I had and be grateful for what I was given. The years had passed, and I'd gotten comfortable being invisible and silent. A nobody in a world where only the elite had the privilege of using magic. I'd grown scared of something that was natural to all of us.

"If you don't like the idea, I can make changes," Evander said. "Everyone gets an input. We're building this thing together. We're a team."

"I claim the roomy cave I uncovered in the east quarter," Stormwing said. "There's enough room in there for Juniper and Cinder."

"Is that a marriage proposal?" Juno stalked in front of Stormwing. "Our baby will need a stable home. Are you a stable dragon? The right dragon to provide care for Cinder?"

Stormwing scales flashed a brilliant yellow. "I'm an excellent provider. Juniper and Cinder will want for nothing."

Juniper laughed, a deep rumble of joy in her broad chest. "I'm sure we'll come to a sensible arrangement. And the cave is delightful." She gently bumped her head against Stormwing's.

I took it all in. My wonderful collection of friends and family. From dragons to witches to rogues, we fit perfectly together. None of us were faultless, but we all had goodness at our centers. And that goodness led us to here. The dragons were back, our enemy defeated, and the realm blossomed again.

"What do you think?" I whispered to Hodgepodge. "Could we make this vision work?"

He sniffed the air. "Do I get my own room?"

"You can have your own house if you like," Evander said. "I've got fifty acres to play with."

I choked out a laugh. "Well, we do need plenty of room for the dragons."

Hodgepodge glared at Finn. "I figure I'll need my own space since the angel hasn't gotten the hint and keeps hanging around us."

"I'll hang around for as long as Bell wants me to." Finn strode over. He leaned down and, in front of everyone, kissed me full on the lips.

Although Hodgepodge hissed and protested, he made no move to stop him. My spiky companion finally realized Finn was determined to stay. And I couldn't be more thrilled.

I turned in a slow circle, taking it all in. This was an outrageously ambitious plan. It would put the realm on the map for all the right reasons. And I'd be in the middle of it, with my friends and family by my side. I caught Emberthorn's gaze and smiled.

"Well, Bell. What will it be?" he asked. "Shall we start a new adventure together this time?"

I nodded, my heartbeat beating out a happy dance of joy. "When do we start?"

# About the author

K.E. O'Connor (Karen) is the author of the whimsical Fireside mysteries, the adorably fun Lorna Shadow cozy ghost mystery series, the wickedly funny Crypt Witch paranormal mystery series, the Magical Misfits Mysteries featuring a sassy cat with a bundle of twisty puzzles to solve, the slightly darker Witch Haven paranormal mystery series featuring four troubled witches and their wonderful furry (feathered and web-slinging companions), and the delicious Holly Holmes cozy baking mysteries.

Stay in touch with the fun mysteries:

**Newsletter:** www.subscribepage.com/cozymysteries
**Website:** www.keoconnor.com
**Facebook:** www.facebook.com/keoconnorauthor

Printed in Great Britain
by Amazon

40308559R00138